Frederick William Robinson

In bad Hands

Vol. III

Frederick William Robinson

In bad Hands
Vol. III

ISBN/EAN: 9783337137304

Printed in Europe, USA, Canada, Australia, Japan

Cover: Foto ©Andreas Hilbeck / pixelio.de

More available books at **www.hansebooks.com**

IN BAD HANDS

AND

OTHER TALES

BY

F. W. ROBINSON

AUTHOR OF

"GRANDMOTHER'S MONEY," "NO CHURCH,"
"THE COURTING OF MARY SMITH,"

ETC., ETC.

IN THREE VOLUMES.

VOL. III.

LONDON:

HURST AND BLACKETT, LIMITED,

13, GREAT MARLBOROUGH STREET.

1887.

CONTENTS

OF

THE THIRD VOLUME.

———

THE STONE BOUQUET.

(CONTINUED.)

B

THE STONE BOUQUET.

CHAPTER III.

THAT ride home was very silent, and almost solemn. The shadows in the carriage seemed part of the gloom about my new life—now that the light of the old, as I have said already, had gone away for good. I was restless and disquieted for all my grave demeanour, and I sat and looked before me and tried to think it out. As if all the thinking in the world could have helped me !

Suddenly, and when we were within a street or two of home, 1 said,

'You never mentioned this Monsieur Danano to me, Cicely.'

My voice roused her. She had fallen into a reverie of her own; after glancing askance at me, once or twice,

'Never?' she rejoined, almost evasively.

'Never,' I repeated.

'But you had heard from father that——'

'I had not heard anything from your father. What had he to tell me?'

'Nothing,' she said, in a low voice.

That was all the conversation between us, until we were in our own dining-room, and were facing each other at an untouched supper. We waited till the servant had gone, having first placed on a side table a bulky packet that had been left at the house during our absence that evening. I rose and stood by the side table whilst I cut the strings of the parcel, which was heavy and unshapely, I remember. This gave me an opportunity of speaking in an unconcerned manner, which I thought might deceive her. As if she did not know my heart better than I did hers.

'Did he speak the truth to-night, that man?' I asked.

'The truth,' she repeated, slowly.

'He said you were an old flame of his.'

'I suppose he liked me a little at one time.'

'You thought he did.'

'Yes, I thought so,' was the naïve confession.

'And he told you so?'

She looked at me steadily for a while. I was sure that she was looking very intently at me, as I went on with my task.

'Yes. But——'

'And you loved him,' I said, turning round and facing her with a darker face than she had seen before; 'why didn't you tell me all the truth? It is not too late to own it. I shall only be sorry that you kept it back from me all this while.'

'Ulric, don't ask me any questions. Cannot the past remain the past between you and me,' she urged; 'what does it matter now it is all over and gone, when he is nothing to me— can never be anything more than what he is now—almost a stranger. Why do you torture me like this?'

'My God! Is it torture to speak of this man?'

'I do not want to speak of him.'

'Did you love him? Why don't you own it frankly?'

'Yes, I did,' she confessed, 'he and I—not much more than boy and girl—would have been man and wife, had not my father separated us. Oh, yes! I loved him, as young girls love the first man who speaks to them as women, and talks of his devotion. But it is all ' gone. Oh, don't you hear me tell you so?'

'Cicely, he loves you still.'

'Oh!'

'And he has told you so to-night. He has reproached you for deceiving him, and you have listened to him. You, my wife—do you hear?'

I had raised my voice now—what demon I looked like then, God knows—but she was huddled in the chair away from me, with her jewelled fingers held before her eyes. I had frightened her—as well I might have done—in my excitement. She could not answer me, and I went on.

'And you love him still. You would have

hissed at him with scorn had the Frenchman been as far away from your heart as I am. I understand it all.'

'No—no. You understand nothing; you are not fair to me, Ulric. I was only a weak girl then —I had not met you, seen you. Why do you make a grievance of all this at last,' she cried, 'when you are going away from me! when you are leaving me alone!'

'That will be no grievance, only a relief,' was my bitter answer; and she sprang up before me then, with her hands drawn from her face, and clenched together; with her eyes blazing with contempt for me, almost with hate.

'You coward!' she cried; then there was a pause, a sudden change of feature, and she fell back in her chair and gave way to a torrent of tears, of passionate sobs, of strange, wild wailings that brought me to my knees, and at her side, in pity for her and the grief I had caused her. I could not see her give way like this and remain uncharitable and exacting. I forgot everything but that she was my fair young wife,

and I had crushed her with my words. I felt
the coward that I was then, and her griefs were
mine again.

'Forgive me, Cicely; think no more of it,' I
implored. 'I was mad or jealous; I will ask no
further questions. It is all past—vanished—
dead! And you *are* my wife. My wife, Cicely,
to whom I have not said a harsh word until to-
night; whom I will trust; who shall not hear a
word of this again, I swear.'

She was moved at last, pacified by degrees;
but she remained very white and sad. The
look in her eyes haunted me for months, as she
rested her thin, hot hands upon my head.

'My poor, foolish old Ulric,' she murmured,
in a low tone, 'who would have thought my
strong, stern husband would have given way
like this.'

'Who would have thought——'

Then I paused—I was silent. I stooped and
kissed her. I had no more to say. The grave,
grey husband was almost himself again.

'There, there, compose yourself, Cicely; I
will not say another word. This is our last

night together for ever and ever so long; we must not look back upon it through our tears.'

'Don't go,' she whispered.

'Oh!—I must go. It is for the best,' I answered, 'it is too late to break my promise.'

She did not speak again. Mechanically I turned to the parcel to give her time to recover from her sorrow, opened it, and drew forth a dark, reddish, heavy mass of stone, at which I looked in amazement for an instant.

'It is the bouquet,' I said at last. 'See, it has come back—a peace-offering, Cicely. We will take it as an omen.'

Cicely glanced at it wonderingly, then shuddered.

A stone bouquet! Its flowers roughly defined still, but with all the poetry gone from it, a hard unmalleable, angular mass. Yes, it was an omen.

CHAPTER IV.

WHEN I was away from her, when we had said
good-bye, when thousands of miles stretched
between my wife and me, I thought of the last
night—that miserable hour of our parting, that
first sharp quarrel between us. I could remember too much, so much that was terrible and
sad—and her troubled face was always before
me. There were so many questions which I
should have liked to ask her now, and her past
was, after all, so unguessed a story. I was
ignorant of it, I was still in the dark; she had
taken me at my word and become impenetrably
silent. I was away, and could not solve my doubts.
I did not speak of them in my letters to her,
and she never alluded again to the trial we had
shared together on the day I went away. Heaven

alone knows how the weeks and months went by in the far-away land where work was arduous and news from home but intermittent. Work did not cure me of the agony of suspense, as work will do at times to a mind ill at ease— it was ever before me to brood upon, and grow like a cancer in my heart, eating away all trust in her. Every letter that I received from her became a study, an effort to detect a difference —the coldness born of our separation from each other, and of *his* proximity to her. He would be always near her, the young, impassionated, handsome suitor—the first love from whom they tore her away—and I, old and grey and defenceless, was in the accursed country whither my ambition had borne me.

Yes, all this is a terrible recital, and yet so commonplace. I was the slave of circumstances —the dupe. They had married her to save her from him—that was the fact which weighed upon me, which bowed my head, and set deep furrows in my cheeks, not the arduous nature of the task to which I was a slave. Yes, always before me—the tear-stained countenance of my

wife, the face of the handsome Frenchman looking into hers, the clash of the band, and the
waltz tune which it played for ever ringing in
my ears, when I found them together, the old
lovers—the hero and heroine of a story which
had been scrupulously kept back, which no one
had cared to tell me lest I should ask too many
questions, and be scared away by the answers
they might give.

There were several French newspapers that
reached the South American quarter wherein I
was prosecuting my work; many of my coadju-
tors were French, whose friends had not forgotten them and sent them news. It was strange
how the one subject engrossed me even in this
particular. With every mail I pored over the
advertisements in the French journals, and when
I saw Danano's name, which was very frequent-
ly, it was an intense relief to me. He was singing in Paris at such and such a time, and here
was my wife's last letter of the same day, with
the London post-mark and dated from her
father's house. They could not be together; it
was all well then!

When Danano was not singing at the opera,
I began to fancy there came no home letters to
me. This was pure fancy, dissipated very often
by a missive from her, but it was a new torture
whilst it lasted, and I grew more crazed upon
it. Thinking it all over now, in this seclusion
where no face I love can look at me, unless it
is down from heaven in pity and forgiveness—
and my mother's face, not hers—I feel sure that
I was mad. After a sunstroke that I had had
and recovered from, I was completely but
quietly and unobtrusively mad, keeping my
madness so completely to myself that those
about me did not even dream that Haviland's
brain was flawed by one idea. I was all business to them when business had grown a horror
to me. My great scheme was, in their estimation, my one thought to which I sacrificed all
health and comfort—when my one thought was
Cicely, the woman I had married and left
—the young wife with a lover in the background watching like a wolf. A man of her
own age, belonging to her romantic past; a
Frenchman with his accursed false French sen-

timent that is ever like an ulcer in their books
and plays and poems.

The climax was reached more speedily than
I had calculated upon. I had made up my mind
to return to England before my time, to leave
to others the reward of success, to let the
world of science and engineering say what it
might of my want of courage to attempt great
works and face great difficulties. I had lived
down ambition and only cared for peace. In a
few months, instead of two more years, I should
be on my way home. I had acted unwisely to
leave home altogether. I should have known
human nature better in my staid middle age.
But this resolve was hastened on more rapidly
than I had bargained for.

There wandered into our camping-ground a
new recruit—a man with high credentials from
his government—a friend of Danano, the actor.
It was this friendship between him and my
wife's old friend that arrested immediately my
attention, although that friendship had not ex-
tended between them to implicit confidence.
This was all the better, or the worse, for me—I

know not which—but it fixed my resolution to
be gone.

Danano was the prince of good fellows, this
man implied, a great genius—a fellow of infinite
jest and infinite sentiment. He was the idol
of the Parisian world, favoured by the aristocracy, flattered by the women, altogether
admirable.

'And so his head is turned by all this adu-
lation?' I inquired, after he had come to the
end of his own encomiums. 'A Frenchman's
head whirls round very quickly with the breath
of praise.'

'Ah, but I do not believe that. Danano is a
man of the world, a sensible being, far-seeing
and acute. He keeps out of mischief,' added
the new-comer, with a laugh, 'but then there
is a reason for it.'

'Ay. Indeed.'

'A *grande passion* which a melancholy Englishman would call an unfortunate attachment.
A first love even, about which he raves—well,
like a genius possibly. That is his one weak-
ness,' added his friend, 'but it keeps him steady

and quiet and out of what you call the hurly-
burly. It has that effect with great men sometimes.'

'He is a sentimentalist.'

'Yes, if you care to call him so.'

'And a sorry one. And the lady's name?'

'Oh, I do not know,' was the reply; 'and, had
I the honour of being acquainted with it, I
should not have considered it my duty to
communicate it to monsieur,' he replied, with
a low bow.

'No, no, of course you would not. And of
course,' I added, with a laugh, 'the lady is
married.'

'Oh! that is the rule all over the world. One
of the two is sure to be married, or where,'
shrugging his shoulders, 'would be the interest
of the story?'

'To a vile Frenchman,' I answered, sharply;
then I left him amazed and indignant and
thinking of pistols.

That evening I was on my way to England.
I left everything in the wildest disorder: I did
not stop to explain; I told no one I was going,

but I threw up my work, cast discredit on my name and good faith, and, with a curt note of resignation on my desk, left the workers to their own devices. They said from that day in the camp that I *was* mad; they knew it more quickly than the dull-witted at home. Danano's friend only thought that I was frightened. I had insulted his countryman and had stolen away to avoid the consequences. An apology would have been sufficient—the Englishman need not have been so frightened as all that.

CHAPTER V.

In London again, and no one aware of my return. That was the grim humour of it. I
caught myself laughing at the idea more than
once in my room at the 'Grosvenor,' but it was a
laugh that told me I was unsafe, there was so
wild a ring in it. I had not hurried back to
the arms of my wife, to the love which might
be waiting for me, to the sure happiness I had
set aside for the fame that I had not secured.
I thought I would wait—that, not being expected, I should have opportunities of discover-
ing the truth, which would be better than living to the end of my days in an atmosphere of
lies. To know the truth and act accordingly.

Was I better than a spy once more—a mean-
spirited, dastardly spy? Perhaps not; but I

do not know the man, beset by the curse of suspicion, who would have acted differently. He
would have found it all out; and it is never a
difficult task when the soul is set on the solving
of the riddle.

For days I watched the house of my father-in-
law, and paid others to watch, picking my spies
up from the street and rewarding them handsomely for any scraps of news they gave me,
and they were not scraps which contained any
news of her. She was away—or she was ill.
A doctor's carriage at the door one morning set
all my plots and plans flying to the winds. I
rushed into the house, announced myself, strode
past the servant into the drawing-room, and
when he had followed me would have caught
him by the throat and squeezed the information
from him, had he not backed to the door in his
alarm.

'Who is ill—is it Mrs. Haviland?—why don't
you tell me? Don't you know who I am?'

'It is—Mr. Haviland—is it not?' gasped
forth the old servant.

'Yes—yes—who is ill, I ask?'

c 2

'My master, sir.'

'That's well. I am glad of that,' I said, to the man's further amazement. 'She is safe, then. Mrs. Haviland is well, I mean? Quite well?'

'I—I don't know, sir.'

'Where is she?'

'I cannot say, Mr. Haviland, really. She is not staying here now.'

I did not answer. Half stunned as I was by the information, I had expected it. I sat down.

'When the doctor has gone, tell Sir William I shall be glad to see him for a few moments.'

'Yes, sir.'

But when the doctor had departed, when he was descending the steps to his carriage, and the footman was holding the open door and looking after him, I stole from the drawing-room and went with swift steps upstairs. The house was familiar to me, and I knew my father-in-law's room. In another instant I had entered unceremoniously and was standing by the sick man's bedside. Sir William stared at me as at an apparition. He was twenty years' older than when I left him.

'Great heaven, Haviland. Is it you?' he cried; 'what has happened? What is it?'

He was very old and feeble, but I did not spare him. I had grown merciless.

'*You* can guess,' I said.

'Cicely! My God—not Cicely. She——'

He stopped and waited for me to explain. And I was baffled.

'I have come to *you* to know what has happened, Sir William,' I said; 'it is I who should hear the news.'

'Yes—but——'

'Where is my wife?'

'At her own home—your home—for what I know to the contrary. Haviland, have you not heard I have been seriously ill—that I am only just recovering? How strange you are.'

'Did she leave you because of your illness?' I asked, bitterly. He looked at me now in grave perplexity of mind. Did he see I was not as sane as when I had bidden him good-bye? Could he have any suspicion of me? I should lose all clue to the truth, if I were not more like my old self. 'You must not mind me, Sir William,' I explained, quite meekly, 'I have been travelling night and day, and am more excited and upset than I ought to be. But I wanted an interview with you—I thought I would come on and see you and Cicely—of course, Cicely—at once. Where is my wife?' I repeated, 'why does she keep away from me?'

'She left here for the country a few weeks ago——'

'You said she was in her own home!' I shouted now.

'She will return to-night to it. That is, I understand she will.'

'You do not know, for certain?'

'Not for certain, Ulric. How should I know anything lying here? How inconsiderate you are!'

'Yes, I am. Forgive me,' I replied. 'You are a sick old man, and I have forgotten that. In what part of the country is she?'

'Folkestone.'

'Folkestone. That is handy for France, Sir William.'

'What do you mean?'

'Is she going on the Continent?'

'I believe not. I do not even know for certain that she is in Folkestone.'

'You do not correspond?'

'N—no, Ulric. Not just at present.'

'Has she written to you?'

'No.'

'Not since she has left this house?'

'Ulric,' pleaded the old man, 'I am not strong enough to talk to you—to answer all your questions. Cicely and I have not agreed very well together of late—we have had a few words— not many,' was the simple correction proffered here; 'don't think, Ulric, it was anything like a quarrel between us. God forbid that. But she was unhappy here; she had grown used to a home of her own, to friends of her own, she said, since her marriage. She has outgrown my ways a little, that is all. And she thought it would be better—and that we should clash less —if she returned to her own establishment.'

'Yes.'

'After people are married, relations *are* better

in the background for awhile. It is an old saying,
Ulric.'

'Yes.'

I could have shrieked at him a thousand
questions now, but I would not put one more to
him. I had become full of a most merciful
consideration for this father lying here sick unto
death. I could have asked him to reconcile his
story of her being at home with her being at
Folkestone; demanded of him the meaning of
her words that she had 'friends of her own;'
asked him if he, a shrewd old man, had objected to those friends; and if one of them—curse
him!—were named Danano? I could have
raved at him like the madman that I was—mad
now with the awful consciousness that my wife
was false to me, that the old lover was once
more in the foreground of her life, and that
I was set apart from her eternally. But I raved
no more. The old man was my friend; I had
always respected him, honoured him. And I
saw he was in trouble.

'I will find Cicely,' I said, calmly, 'in a day
or two, at any rate. Good-bye, Sir William,

and better health to you. I am sorry I have been so hasty, but I have been very anxious.'

Then I went out of the room and shut the door softly behind me.

CHAPTER VI.

It was night when I went to my own home. I took time to consider it all out. I would do nothing more in haste. People were becoming suspicious. Even the servants I met upon the staircase of the hotel seemed to be glancing askance at me. I do not know why—unless the muttering in my room had reached their ears.

The servant who admitted me was the man I had left in charge. It was his turn to be surprised.

'Mr. Haviland!' he exclaimed.

'Yes. I have come back.'

He looked out into the wet street—I remember it was raining hard—for a cab heaped up with luggage, or some sign of a traveller's return, and then at me, standing there in evening dress. I passed him and went into my own house. It looked very desolate.

'When does your mistress come back from —Folkestone?' I inquired.

'We expect her back by a late train, sir,' he replied: 'she sent a telegram to the housekeeper this morning.'

'I should be glad to surprise her, Robert,' I said, with a pleasant, hearty laugh—not one of the new laughs which made people turn white to listen to me!—'this must be a secret between you, and me, and the housekeeper, if you will. No one else.'

'Does not mistress know that——'

'I am supposed to be in South America,' I interrupted, 'so this will be an agreeable surprise for her. I rely on your confidence. Don't forget. I shall reward you presently and— handsomely.'

The man chuckled at my little plan. He was a dull fellow, without a grain of intelligence. On that night I was a better actor than Danano.

'Where shall I go?' I said, half thoughtfully.

'Your own study will be best, sir,' suggested the man.

'Yes, capital.'

'Mistress never goes into it,' he explained. 'I don't think the room has been opened for three months, sir. I had better light a fire.'

'No. Bring me a lamp, and leave it as it is. And—take no further notice of me under any circumstances. You understand?'

'Yes, sir; I understand.'

I passed upstairs into my old study; it was thick with dust. No one had thought of it, or attended to it of late days. It was like a dead room. Well, I was dead to her, and not expected back any more. And the servants had neglected it in the mistress's absence, and —like the mistress. On the mantelpiece was the stone bouquet. It was a fitting emblem after all. I took it up and poised it in my hand. How heavy it seemed to have grown, or had I become weaker? It was like an ugly iron ornament rusting away, and felt like iron to my touch. When the servant had brought the

lamp, I locked myself in. I would not be surprised. Then I sat down and waited, and stared
at the stone bouquet, and thought of all that
had happened since I had sat there last in that
room, of every miserable fact in my purposeless
life.

Presently—two hours afterwards, it might be
—there was a knocking and ringing at the
outer door. I unlocked my study and listened.
There were voices talking in the hall downstairs
—men's voices.

'She has not reached home yet?' I heard some
one inquire.

'No sir, not yet.'

I knew the voice, and I came out on the
landing-place and craned my face over the
balusters to look at him. Had he glanced up,
a face grinning out of a coffin would have
dismayed him less.

'I will wait.'

'But——'

'No—I will write a note. Please see that
Madame has it immediately upon her arrival.'

I heard money clink in the servant's palm, as

Monsieur Danano was shown into a little room
on the right of the door. I went back to the
study and waited very patiently. I could be
very patient when I chose. 'Everything comes
to him who waits.' The line runs in that fashion
somewhat.

Presently I heard the street door close after
Monsieur Danano, and the servant stood in the
hall as if he were thinking, and with his finger
nails pressed to his lips. When he went away,
I stole downstairs into the room wherein Danano
had been shown. It was a favourite little room
of my wife's, looking on the square. The gas
was burning there. On the desk in the corner
was a sealed letter. I dashed at it, tore it open,
and read amidst many wild words of affection
and fool's rhapsody these words of warning:

*' You must hesitate no longer. I will come at
twelve for you, my beloved. It is too late for
further deliberation. We must fly. Your husband
is in London, and dangerous.'*

Dangerous! How did he know that I was
dangerous?

I put the letter in another envelope, sealed it, and left it on the davenport whence I had picked it up. It might be as well to see the end of this, the very, very end. I went up to my study again, and sat there with the stone bouquet clutched in my hands, as if some need of comfort, or of self-restraint, might come from its cold touch. But the life-blood at my temples was like the fluttering of a bird, and my heart was swelling and leaping with sickening force within me, and everything before me was shimmering through a mist of blood, as though a red veil had been cast before my eyes.

So I knew all at last. It had all been true enough then. There was no further doubts for me. This could not end like the last act of a comedy, with explanations, forgiveness, and flippant jesting over past mistakes. The dark curtain must drop on the grimmest tragedy by which a man's life can be shadowed. I was not the first man to be deceived—or the last man to avenge deceit. Not by many thousands, I thought, laughing again at the crowds of fools who were like me, who were about me too, and grinning at me. I could see their faces—and their awful eyes—everywhere that night.

There came another knocking and ringing at the door. It was she. She had come home at last. God! I could hear her voice in the hall.

I stole out on to the landing again. I had the stone bouquet still in my hand, and that was very strange. The servant was speaking to her, telling her of the last visitor who had called.

'Where is his letter?' I heard her ask.

'In the morning-room, madam.'

She passed in, and the servant lingered in the hall. Once he looked up the well-staircase, but he did not see me watching. I had lowered the gas outside the study door, and was standing somewhat back, wondering myself what I was going to do next.

Her voice in the hall once more recalled me from my half-stupor.

'Don't remove the boxes from the cab,' she was saying hurriedly, 'leave all as it is, Robert—tell the man to wait. I—I am called away again—at once.'

She was coming upstairs towards me. On the second stair, she paused and looked back at the servant.

'I have written a letter—give it to Monsieur Danano when he returns. He will understand.'

No—he will never understand in this world, neither will Cicely Haviland, nor her mad husband. It is all left for the next. As she came upstairs, I sprang forward and struck at her from the darkness of my lair, and she fell back, with one little cry, a dead woman on the marble pavement of the hall.

I had killed her with the stone bouquet.

They do not know at the asylum that I am writing this. They will see it presently and it may amuse them—or it may hang me. It matters not which. I suppose I am mad now— very mad. But it was not Cicely's death that turned my brain, or wholly wrecked it. That seemed just enough till I read the letter she had left for Danano, and which I had thought was her instructions where to meet him. It was that letter which drove me raving mad. Only ten lines, and yet to bring me to this. They are seared into my soul till the judgment-day.

'*I will not see you. Have I been hiding from you all this while and for so poor a sequel? I go away again to escape you—to wait fearlessly for my husband and to confess the truth to him. To confess that I was a weak vain woman, yes; one who loved you, yes; but guilty, never. And so God will forgive us both in His good time perhaps, and as my husband will. I will pray for it very hard. Farewell, Louis, and for ever. I begin my new life—my better life—from this night.*'

She was right. Before the ink was hardly dry, she had begun life anew.

THE FOURTH SON OF THE EARL
OF MOO.

THE FOURTH SON OF THE EARL OF MOO.

————

THE Reverend Paul Ledwitch was fathoms deep in the perusal of his *Times* newspaper, and the Reverend Paul Ledwitch's mother-in-law was fathoms deep in wool-work of some kind or other, and flourishing, twisting, and twirling two highly-polished wooden skewers in that energetic way for which she had been invariably distinguished. Mrs. Goodfields was an energetic woman, under whose feet the grass was not disposed to grow, and her son-in-law would have been knee-deep in grass had he been left to himself and allowed to have his own way, which before and after the decease of Mrs. Ledwitch *née* Goodfields—Arabella Araminta Goodfields, who had had almost as much energy as her mother—had never been the case.

This was fortunate for the Reverend Paul Ledwitch, for he wanted rousing, and Mrs. Goodfields, by a merciful dispensation of Providence, was a natural rouser. He would be at peace with all the world, and his mother-in-law was seldom at peace with one person in it of her acquaintance, not even with the members of Mr. Ledwitch's own congregation, with whom she quarrelled in turn for not treating her with 'proper respect.' Mrs. Goodfields was an austere woman of aristocratic descent— second cousin to an Irish viscount who was living quietly abroad out of the way of his creditors— and therefore she *had* something to be proud of; Mr. Ledwitch was a lethargic, placable man, who composed sermons very much of the same character as himself, and whose natural bent was catching butterflies. The composition of his sermons was a moral torture and a mental strain upon him, just as the understanding of them afterwards was to his broad-faced,

bovine Lincolnshire flock in the little village of
Deepdunes—population three hundred and four,
and two babies expected before the first of
September—but show him butterflies, let them
flutter in his way over the broad, flat, green
meadows stretching around his dumpty little
church, and he verged upon genius. He was
lachrymose and monotonous in his pulpit, but in
the meadows, in his straw hat, and with a blue
gauze bag at the end of a long cane, he was almost a giddy boy. He was a free man then—
free of Mrs. Goodfields who ruled him with a
rod of iron.

The late Mrs. Ledwitch, it was rumoured in
Deepdunes, had ruled him with the same
objectionable article of domestic discipline, and
hence catching moths and butterflies, studying
their manners and customs, diving into the
inner life of their wriggling and hairy progeni-
tors the caterpillars, had been as it were a
harbour of refuge from many a storm to the
Reverend Paul Ledwitch, until it had pleased
Heaven to remove his helpmate, for whom he
grieved as deeply as though she had been a

more amiable and loving woman than she was.

Whether it was out of respect to his late wife, or whether it was in sheer subjection to a stronger will than his own, or whether, as sardonic folk were not slow to assert—there were at least four 'sardonics' in Deepdunes—it was on account of a snug little bit of property which Mrs. Goodfields had the power to will to whomsoever she chose, that accounted for her sojourn at the vicarage, certain it was that Mrs. Goodfields who had made her son-in-law's house her own during her daughter's lifetime, continued to constitute it her abiding place after that lady's decease. And there she was, that bright July morning, particularly at home, and her grey-haired son-in-law of forty-one perusing his newspaper, which always turned up at Deepdunes twenty-four hours after publication, owing to cross-country roads and a general difficulty in reaching the village, which was well out of the way of any railway station, and very nearly well out of the world.

'Is there nothing in the paper this morning, Mr. Ledwitch, absolutely nothing?' asked Mrs.

Goodfields, briskly at last. A little too briskly,. but he did not notice it.

'No news of any importance that I can see,' he replied, without taking his eyes from it.

'You have been an hour-and-a-half—to my certain knowledge—buried in it,' remarked Mrs Goodfields, 'and you haven't opened your lips the whole time.'

'Haven't I? Well, I did not remark that,' he said, looking up at last with a feeble kind of smile that always aggravated his late wife's mother.

'What *have* you been reading?'

'I hardly remember. Oh! by the way, there *is* something interesting,' he exclaimed; 'a full report of the entomological——'

'My dear sir, don't tell me anything about that. Please do not. I ask it as a favour,' she said, holding up her hands full of wool and knitting pins.

'Certainly, Mrs. Goodfields—certainly.'

'Have you looked over the Births, Deaths, and Marriages this morning?' she inquired.

'I have not—at present.'

'Just like you. Friends may be born, buried and—bridalled without a human being knowing what has happened to them. Why do you neglect that part of the paper, and——'

'I'm not neglecting it, Mrs. Goodfields. I am coming to it directly.'

'I don't believe you would have thought of such a thing, if I had not mentioned it.'

'Oh! come now,' said Mr. Ledwitch, helplessly.

He probably would have left that task to Mrs. Goodfields, having an expedition on his mind to Claycross Dyke, where a wonderful specimen of *Vanessa Io* had been seen as late as yesterday afternoon. The gardener's boy had called it 'old spotty,' but Mr. Ledwitch knew what he meant perfectly well. And there could be nothing in the first column worth his looking at, he knew; he had forgotten all his friends, or they had forgotten him, long ago, and he was not deeply interested in Mrs. Goodfields' friends, whose high-sounding names, and whose important places in the world, were dinned into his ears with irritating frequency. He glanced at the notices listlessly—with fishy grey eyes and an expression bordering on idiocy, and then he gave a sudden leap in the air—almost an acrobatic leap—and brought the heart into the mouth of his mother-in-law, who was totally unprepared for such excitement from a human being naturally undemonstrative.

'Gracious heavens!' he exclaimed, 'mercy upon us! What can it possibly mean?'

'What can *what* mean?'

'I don't see the object—I don't make it out. I——' and here the Reverend Paul Ledwitch put his right elbow on his knee, and his hand to his head, and sat in deep thought with the newspaper trailing in front of him, till Mrs. Goodfields snatched it out of his left hand, and frightened him by her impulsive course of action.

'What is it?' she asked.

'In the Marriages,' he replied; 'it's—it's astounding. You might have knocked me down with a——Have you found it?'

'No; I haven't. But I will,' and Mrs. Goodfields set on her nose a massive gold-framed pair of eyeglasses, and firmly focussed the intelligence.

She had soon discovered the piece of news
which had surprised Mr. Ledwitch, and which
corrugated her expansive brow, and made her
thin lips shut with a snap like a mousetrap.
Then she opened her mouth again, and read
aloud with deliberate emphasis the following :—

'*On the 13th inst., at St. Mark's, Deepdunes,
Lincolnshire, by the Rev. Paul Ledwitch, M.A., the
Honourable Septimus Bullthorpe, fourth son of the
Earl of Moo, of Moo Hall, South Wales, to Alice
Henrietta Shotter, only daughter of the late
Timothy Shotter, of Tiger House, Camberwell Park,
S.E.*'

'What do you make of that, Mr. Ledwitch?'
she asked.

'I don't make anything of it, my dear madam.
I can't.'

'Have you the faintest idea?'

'No; I haven't.'

'You never had,' she replied, smartly. 'This
is a hoax.'

'Yes; I am aware it's a hoax. I have not
married anyone for three weeks. The last

couple were Buncle, the wheelwright, and Sally Walker.   And Buncle had his face tied up, poor fellow.'

'It's an infamous hoax,' asserted his mother-in-law, without any regard for Buncle.

'It is, Mrs. Goodfields.   It is.'

'And what are you going to do?'

'Well, I haven't made up my mind just at present.'

'It must be detected and exposed.'

'That will be my duty, of course.   I will write to the *Times* before the post goes out.'

'You will do nothing of the kind, sir,' said Mrs. Goodfields, snappishly.

'Eh—dear me.   Why not?'

'At least, not yet.   The mischief is done, I daresay—but we must assert our innocence to the parties most intimately concerned.'

'Certainly.   The child unborn is not more——'

'You must write to the Earl of Moo.'

'Ye—es; it might be as well.'

'And to the Honourable Septimus Bullthorpe.'

'Ye—es; and to him too, I suppose,' he added, with a sigh.

'And to Miss Alice Henrietta Shotter—no, I would not write to her; doubtless, she is at the bottom of this gigantic fraud upon the public, if the truth could be elucidated. Paul Ledwitch,' she said, solemnly, 'you must elucidate the truth.'

'I fancy, after all, that a letter to the *Times* would be the better way of making things plain.'

'That can be done—that will be done in due course,' she said, solemnly. 'But it is your duty to call upon this Miss Shotter, or the Shotter relatives, and ascertain what the motive is, or the deep design, and unearth it for the sake of the dignity of the house of Moo. It will be the means of introducing you to the notice of the Earl of Moo—it may advance you in the Church presently, who can tell. And goodness knows you need advancement, Mr. Ledwitch. You've stuck here long enough. If you had the spirit of a mouse in you—which you have not—you would start for South Wales this very evening, and see the Earl of Moo at once.'

'I really think that a letter to the *Ti*——'

'But you will not go to South Wales, of course.'

'I will write to his lordship.'

'That is imperative.   And to the son.'

'Yes.   Although a letter to the *Ti*——'

'It would have shown a greater respect to the aristocracy of this land, whose names have been thus cruelly trifled with and thrust into unbecoming and unsought-for publicity, if you had paid them a personal interview, however great the inconvenience might be to you.'

'I'm sure that a letter to the *Ti*——'

'Will put the conspirators on their guard, and enable them to elude detection,' she concluded. 'And such a gross imposition as this must be discovered and punished.'

'It certainly is an exceedingly base and cruel trick,' said the Reverend Paul Ledwitch, warming with his subject.

'It is.'

'But I think the *Ti*——'

'The Earl of Moo, or his son, will write to the newspapers.   That is their business.'

'Yes.   So it is.'

'But they may not see it. They may be abroad.'

'So they may.'

'And this Shotter——'

'My dear madam, Miss Shotter may be the injured party for what we know to the contrary. The blow, for some sinister purpose, may be aimed at the defenceless bosom of Miss Shotter.'

'I don't believe it for an instant.'

'It is at present a complete mystery.'

'Which we will unravel, Paul.'

'If it's possible—certainly,' assented her son-in-law.

But the unravelling of the mystery was not so readily done as contemplated. Not all the energetic nature of Mrs. Goodfields, exclusively directed as it was to the rousing of the vicar of Deepdunes, was sufficient to explain the motives which had actuated some person or persons unknown to register in the columns of a newspaper that the Reverend Paul Ledwitch had officiated at a marriage which by no possibility could have come off as advertised.

The Reverend Paul Ledwitch wrote to the
Earl of Moo, and to his cub of a son—as he
disparagingly termed him afterwards—the Honourable Septimus Bullthorpe, but to neither
epistle was the slightest reply vouchsafed; he
wrote to the *Times* at last, and had his letter
published therein, without any effect upon the
mind of any human being that was apparent;
and it was not till he came across a chance advertisement in the papers informing the British
public that the Earl of Moo would preside on
Saturday afternoon next at a public meeting at
Exeter Hall in aid of the funds for the Propa-
gation of the Gospel among Hairdressers, that
Mr. Ledwitch became aware that here was the
mystery still intact and unexplained, and to be
confronted now or never.

'You will go to London at once, Mr. Ledwitch,' said his mother-in-law, 'and see his
lordship—and see the Shotters. They are all
together in town.'

'Ye—es, they are all in town, I expect.'

'Then, there you've got them.'

'Oh, yes—I've got them.'

'This is a case in which your name has been called in question—taken in vain, Paul, I may say,' she remarked, 'and it must be seen into. It may be a conspiracy levelled at you—who can tell?'

'Yes, I think I'll go,' said Mr. Ledwitch; 'I have a little business in town next week, at the Clerical Stores, but I may as well go this week instead.'

'To be sure. I'll see your portmanteau is packed immediately.'

Hence it was that on the morning of the Friday, Mr. Ledwitch started for London, determined to sift the mystery to the bottom—to leave not a stone unturned to satisfy the curiosity of his mother-in-law and himself. He had certainly got roused to an inquiry stage at last. There must have been some motive in expending six or eight shillings on a bogus advertisement—people did not fling away shillings for nothing—and the object was to annoy him, or Miss Shotter, or the Earl of Moo, or the son of the Earl of Moo. The odd part of the whole affair was, he could not tell which party it was intended to annoy.

When he was in town and had had his dinner at the Inns of Court Hotel, it began to dawn upon him that he had probably come upon a wild-goose expedition, and he wished in his heart that he had *not* been roused, but that he was trotting about in the Lincolnshire fens with his gauze bag after the butterflies, or his bull's-eye lantern, at the hour of midnight, after the moths. He would have been happy there—and, after all, what did it matter to him, any more than to the other parties mentioned, and who evidently treated the whole affair with silent contempt. He was afraid he should look like a fussy old parson meddling with business that hardly concerned him, and dragging into light again a matter that everyone had been glad to forget at the earliest possible opportunity. He thought it would be advisable to proceed cautiously . . . . He would take a little stroll over to Camberwell in the early hours of that summer evening, and interview Miss Shotter in the first instance. Perhaps after that there would be no necessity to call upon the Earl of Moo before or after his Presidency at Exeter Hall to-

E 2

morrow afternoon; he did not particularly like the idea of calling upon the Earl of Moo, a right honourable lord of the land, who had not taken the trouble to answer his letter.

Now that he came to consider the matter coolly and temperately, and without the goading influence of his mother-in-law, he was quite certain that he did *not* like the idea. He was placing himself in a false position with the Earl of Moo, he was afraid, and subjecting himself to a snub from his lordship for his extra officiousness. And yet there might be a desperate and deeply-laid conspiracy in the background—the advertisement must have meant something—there must have been somebody working in the dark and for some out-of-the-way reason or other. He could go to Camberwell Gate by an Atlas omnibus for twopence, and by a tramcar for a penny the rest of the way to Camberwell Park, a topographical waiter had informed him. The whole mystery might be solved for the modest outlay of sixpence there and back—the Shotters would be sure to know more about it than he did, and the Shotters were located at

Tiger House, Camberwell Park, S.E. He would proceed to Camberwell forthwith, and make every inquiry for Miss Shotter.

He found that he had some trouble to find Tiger House. It took a lot of finding. The cabmen recommended him to try Tiger Bay, and Tiger Yard, and Tiger Rents, and though each and all of these localities looked as if any amount of conspiracies—or of anything else—might be conveniently hatched there, they did not associate well, neither they nor their surroundings, with the Earl of Moo, or the Honourable Septimus Bullthorpe. Tiger House, Mr. Ledwitch had conjectured, might be probably a seminary for young ladies—and the plot had been the outcome of the teeming, mischievous minds of boarding-school girls—but there was no school with so unpleasant an appellation in the vicinity.

The Reverend Paul Ledwitch got his information at last from the police-station at the corner of the Camberwell New Road, and was subjected to a close scrutiny from a member of the official force on duty at the time.

'Yes, I know Tiger House. What do *you* want there?'

Mr. Ledwitch felt he was not being treated with a fair amount of civility.

'I don't think I am called upon to state my business,' he said, with no little display of dignity.

'Oh! it's business—is it? You know old Shotter, do you?'

'I don't know old Shotter, or any Shotter. I thought Shotter was dead.'

'Tim Shotter's dead, and,' he added, after a thoughtful pause, 'a thundering good job too. He gave us a lot of trouble—and we never could lay hold of him. Never.'

'You—you don't mean to say that these Shotters are not—are not respectable?' asked the Vicar of Deepdunes.

'I don't say anything about their being respectable. But if you are—I should advise you to be cautious. You are a clergyman really?'

'I am.'

'Have you lost a dog?'

'No, I haven't,' replied the surprised vicar.

'One of our men will put you in the way.
And he can wait outside till you come out.'

'Good gracious!' exclaimed Mr. Ledwitch,
'is there any danger?'

'I don't say there is,' replied the reserved
policeman; 'I don't say but what everybody
has come out who ever went in—if not always
in the same condition. Not always.'

'I do not follow you, my good man. Am I
safe in going to Tiger House?'

'I don't say you ain't. Here, Jem.'

Jem appeared. Unmistakably, a policeman
in private dress, with a billycock hat all on one
side, and champing at the stalk of a strawberry.

'Show this gent round to Shotter's, Jem.
Business, he says.'

Was the Reverend Paul Ledwitch deceived,
or did the speaker wink at the new-comer on
the scene? It was a keep-your-eye-upon-him
warning, and he was under suspicion. It was
very ridiculous. As if he should have called at
a police-station, if he were in any degree connected with a nefarious transaction—as if he

looked nefarious. He would follow the matter
to the end now; he was glad he had called.
There was a mystery, but he was on his guard.
There were adventure too and incident—and all
the adventures and incidents of his previous
career had been connected with moths and
butterflies. What a deal he should have to tell
Mrs. Goodfields when he got back to Lincolnshire, to be sure!

He walked by the side of his guide, who
slouched round to the back of Camberwell Park
and then dived into various small thoroughfares,
turning up at last before a row of shops in a
narrow street which in the distance seemed to
end in a strip of water, some timber yards and
whitening works, and in which street legions of
dirty children were whooping and yelling, playing and fighting.

'There's Shotter's,' said Jem. 'I daresay
you'll find me about here when you come out
again—if you're not too long.' The Reverend
Paul Ledwitch surveyed Shotter's from the
other side of the way, and did not like the look
of it. Shotter—old Shotter—did not keep his

place clean, and it was necessary to keep a place clean when the stock-in-trade consisted of canary-birds, finches and linnets, pigeons, bantam cocks and hens, parrots and magpies, a monkey or two, rabbits and guinea-pigs, and innumerable dogs. Shotter was evidently a naturalist, and his emporium could be smelt across the road with startling distinctness. It was a small house, with some of the windows of the first floor broken and stuffed with rags. TIGER HOUSE, in black capitals on a drab background, was painted between the windows, and SHOTTER was emblazoned over the shop front in a dusky red.

Shotter was a respectable tradesman, one who probably did a fair amount of business as a naturalist, judging by his miscellaneous wares. He, the Reverend Paul Ledwitch, saw nothing to arouse suspicion in the emporium of Mr. Shotter, or to warrant his receiving from the police a subdued warning to be careful when engaged in business transactions with its proprietor.

'I wonder what is my next step,' he solilo-

quised, as he crossed the road to the shop,
which smelt stronger with every step towards
it, and had all the richness of aroma of a stale
menagerie when he was fairly on the premises.

To his surprise Mr. Shotter himself, a dwarf
of a man in stature, but tremendously wide to
make up for it, loomed before him in his shirt-
sleeves—and very dirty shirt-sleeves they were.
He was wearing a sealskin cap well over his
brows, and smoking a short clay pipe.

'Oh, you've come at last, have you, mister?'
he exclaimed, in a hoarse, grating voice; 'not
that *I* was in a hurry for you. But blest if you
ain't a-took your time for all that.'

'Did you expect me before, then?'

'You're the parson, ain't you?'

'Yes, I am a minister, but——'

'Then you'd better hook it upstairs afore she
goes off altogether. It's no use a-jawin' to me,
is it? I didn't send for you,' he said. 'I had
enuf to do with one of your lot when I had
five years penal for wot I didn't do—oh, you
know all about it—fast enuf, everybody
knows. I don't pay rates and taxes to be civil

to anybody, and if you've thought better on it, an' come here after all, *I* ain't called upon to thank you, am I?   I didn't want you—and the sooner you're gone agin the better.'

Mr. Ledwitch was bewildered by this torrent of vituperative eloquence.   There was no time to reply, and Mr. Shotter did not pause for a reply.   An explanation would have been more to the purpose, but Mr. Shotter did not leave him any room for explanations, any time for the collecting of his ideas, so that he might calmly and deliberately state his case.   And Mr. Shotter had been drinking, and, though the smell of rum was a pleasant and odoriferous contrast to that of the live stock, it was hardly worth arguing with a 'rum customer.'

And the opportunity did not present itself, Mr. Shotter flung open a door on which hung cages of several birds, who summarily toppled off their perches and chirped and fluttered in much confusion as he swung it open.   He put a half-closed red hand to his mouth and shouted at the very top of his lungs,

'Sophy.'

'Hullo,' responded a voice as gruff as his own from remote regions above stairs, 'what's the row now?'

'Here's the bloomin' parson thought better on it.   He's comin' up sharp.'

Mr. Ledwitch hesitated no longer.   It was useless to enter into any explanation, and up-stairs was some poor soul sick unto death.   He ascended a steep flight of uncommonly rickety stairs, holding on for precaution's sake to a greasy hand-rail, which was broken in one or two places and stuck out here and there in javelin fashion, bristling with splinters.   At the top of the stairs were two doors; the one looking into a back room was open, the front room over the shop was locked, and the key in the trousers pocket of the gentleman down-stairs. Mr. Ledwitch walked into the back room, took off his hat and looked round.

It was a small apartment, and did not take much looking round to master the position.   It was a room that was a bit of surprise to the vicar of Deepdunes, for it was a clean and neatly, if poorly, furnished apartment, without any sign

of the dirt and squalor which characterised the
rest of the establishment. There was a small
harmonium in the corner, there was a youngish
woman of thirty, with a complexion of chrome
yellow, standing by the fireplace, and in the little
iron bedstead by the window lay a girl of some
eighteen years of age, very pallid, very thin,
very handsome, with great dark staring eyes,
and a wealth of dark hair streaming over the
pillow on which her head was resting. She lay
very still; there was a faint quivering of the
eyelashes as Mr. Ledwitch entered, which might
have been taken as a greeting or not according
to the strength of the imagination of the visitor,
and there was a look of surprise that followed by
degrees, as if she could not believe the evidence
of her own dark eyes. The woman with the
yellow face, and with as fine a specimen of a
scowl impressed upon that yellow as Mr. Ledwitch had ever seen in his life, put her hands
upon her hips and exclaimed harshly and unceremoniously:

'And who the devil are you?'

'I am a minister of the Church of England,'

was the answer; ' can I be of any service here?'

' What's he sent you for? Is he afraid to trust himself with the likes of us now—or what?' asked the yellow woman.

Mr. Ledwitch thought that he would not explain to this inquisitive personage, and that it might be difficult to explain. The white face of the sick girl attracted him, and the sad earnest expression upon it enlisted his sympathy. He was a man naturally sympathetic, was the Reverend Paul Ledwitch, but in Deepdunes there was not much opportunity of expressing kindness and tenderness. Everybody was deplorably dull and disgustingly healthy.

' Have you come instead of Mr. Mandeville?' said the soft voice from the bed.

' I heard downstairs that you had sent for a minister,' he answered. ' I do not know Mr. Mandeville.'

' It is chance then?'

' Partly chance. But I was coming to see you.'

Again the great dark eyes betrayed surprise, and for a while there was silence in the room.

The invalid was thinking deeply; the yellow young woman was watching her askance, varying proceedings by furtive glances towards the new comer. Presently the eyes of the sick girl closed, and the colour left her lips, and the face took a shade more pallor and more angularity to itself. The woman went to the bedside.

'There!' she said; 'she's off again—off and on—faint after faint; it's enough to tire a horse out. She'd better die and get it over sharp, I'm thinking. What do you say about it?'

Mr. Ledwitch did not quite know what to say, and looked it.

'What's she got to live for? With her straight-laced notions, and her voice all gone to pieces, and the guv'nor dead against all she says and does. She'd better *cut* it. I only wish I was in her place, that's all!'

'That is a hard thought for one so young as you are.'

'I've had my turn,' was the short reply. 'I don't want to get old, and I won't either. Look at the beastly colour I am—that's the jarndice, that is. And it gets worse and worse.'

And here the discontented female walked to a small dressing-glass on the toilet-table, critically examined her complexion, and then lumped herself down, in a despairing fashion, in a cane-bottomed chair.

'I *am* cussed ugly, and no kid about it,' she remarked.

'This poor child here ; had you not better——'

'Oh, let her be. She'll come round again in a jiffey—in a minute or two, that is ; she does it on purpose, just to get me savage. She—oh, Alice, old girl, do pull yourself together,' she exclaimed, with a dash across the room towards the invalid ; 'don't make it so beastly hard for me. Don't go and die right off. I didn't mean that exactly. Don't——'

Alice had opened her eyes again and was looking at her dreamily.

'Oh! here you are,' continued the woman. 'Now, then, what's to be done with this old geyser ? Let's have it.'

The sick girl looked towards the Reverend Paul Ledwitch.

'What has brought you here, sir ?' she asked.

' I will not trouble you about it now, my child,' said the vicar, kindly. 'You are too ill to be disturbed by any business of mine; and such paltry little business as it is.'

'Perhaps Sophy will do as well. She's very quick, very kind, and only a little rough. She's like a sister to me in everything.'

'Sister, indeed!' was the gruff correction; ' no, nor half a sister. We don't want any lies about it. I'm her cousin—old Shotter's gal —and a precious bad one too. Anybody'll tell you that; and I don't care who does!'

'I don't think it's worth troubling you either, Miss Shotter,' said Mr. Ledwitch, politely, 'and, at all events, some other time will do. But,' turning to the invalid, 'might I ask, before I go, why you sent for a minister?'

'He had a good opinion of me once, when I was in his choir, sixteen months ago,' she said, thoughtfully; 'but uncle would not let me stop after father died.'

'Why not?'

'He thought my voice was good enough for the music-halls.'

'Oh!' exclaimed Mr. Ledwitch—'great heavens!'

'So it was,' muttered Sophy, 'a blessed sight
too good.'

'And you sang at—at one of those dreadful
places?' said Mr. Ledwitch.

'I had to get my living, sir.'

'Yes. But, my poor girl, there are many
ways——'

'Here, hold hard, parson,' interrupted Sophy,
very bluntly now. 'She's not a poor girl; she's
a good one, and has kept herself straight and
proper all her life—straighter and properer than
you, I'll bet. She's the best of us, I must
say. We've all run wild a bit but Alice; we're
a bad lot, bar one. And you needn't think
a word that's wrong of her; put it all down
to me, and you won't be far out in your
reckoning.'

'I am not thinking wrong of your cousin, or
of you,' he added.

'I'm a music-hall party too. I do the comic
biz, and the dancing, and the *topical*, and don't
get on at any of it. I ain't up to much. Some-

times they hoot me at the " Rosemary and the
Star" when I lay it on too thick. What's the
odds of that now I've got such a frightful
colour? But Alice here does the sentimental,
and gets a turn or two at the " Pav." and the
"Troc." now and then. Oh, fine!'

. Sophy Shotter was talking Hebrew to the
vicar. But he said very mildly to her sick
cousin :

'And you liked this kind of life ?'

'No,' answered the girl, with a shiver, ' I
hated it.'

' I'm very glad to hear it.'

'Oh, shut up !' said Sophy, restlessly.

'And I did want to tell the minister so, if—if
anything happened to me. For he believed in
me once. He was a good man. He was sorry
when I took to the halls. He—he thought the
very worst of me afterwards. Oh, dear !'

'That's just it,' cried Sophy, ' as if we're all
bad. That's why I should have liked to shy
something at his head, instead of sneaking
round to his house to-day and begging and
praying him to come and see Alice. As if *she*

wasn't good—a blessed sight better than he is.
As if she couldn't have married Spoffins—you've
heard of Spoffins, the giant comic, I suppose?'

'No, I cannot say I have.'

'My stars! you must have been dragged up
in a desert, old man. Not heard of Spoffins?
Why, he gets fifty quid a week all round. But
she couldn't abear him.'

'Indeed,' said Mr. Ledwitch, politely, 'and so
comic too.'

'And if she'd been fly, and played her cards
well, everybody knows she could have nobbled
a real lord's son. He *was* an awful fool, certainly—oh, goodness! and an awful wretch.
But, at any rate, he would have made a lady of
her, and that's——'

'Sophy, Sophy!' exclaimed Alice, 'you must
not talk like that. You know I—cannot bear
it.'

'Here, don't go off again. I'll stash it; I
haven't any more to say. That's the only thing
we've ever had a row about, she and I; and,
my eye, an all-round row it was. As if anything wasn't better than this life; as if a

brougham and lots of coin to spend, and a
slobbering idiot to help you spend it, wasn't
ever so much better than being knocked about
by the old brute downstairs.'

'Your father, does he——'

'Pitch into us?' concluded Sophy. 'Oh, yes,
when we put him out or don't give him enough
money to get drunk with. I'm used to it. I
can give him as good as he sends ; but, when he
lays a hand on this little one here, I feel as if I
could almost put a knife into him.'

'Horrible, horrible !' exclaimed the astonished
vicar.

'Yes, he is. That's exactly it. Ah, and one
of these fine days he'll go too far, you see.
And mind you, Alice girl, if you go and die, I'll
up and tell how he threw you down all those
blessed stairs because you wouldn't ask the
Bull-pup to lend you twenty pounds. There,
that's the fact, old man: the gov'nor thought
Alice was flinging away a good chance of
bettering herself with the Bull-pup, and he
wasn't far out about that.'

'Might I enquire who—who is the Bull-pup ?'

'Oh, a real lord's son, to be sure. The girls call him Bull-pup; it isn't a bad name for him.'

'Is his real name Septimus Bullthorpe?'

'That's the party.

> " He's a nobleman's son,
> He's a nobleman's son,
> He's——"

But what do *you* know about him?'

'I will explain to-morrow. I will come to-morrow and see how your cousin is. And I should like the address of the doctor who attends her, and Mr. Mandeville's address. My child,' he said, leaning over the sick girl, ' if I could do anything for you, in any way to help you, I should be very glad.'

'You're very kind, sir,' came the low answer back, ' but I don't know of anything just now.'

'I may come again to see how you are?'

'You are going to Mr. Mandeville's?'

'Yes.'

'If uncle will let you come again I should, I think, like to hear what Mr. Mandeville says about me now,' she said, in a low voice.

'I will come again.'

Then Mr. Ledwitch departed, and Sophy Shotter, closing the door behind her, came a few stairs down with him.

'The doctor's name is Dolby: the minister's house is by his church, next street. If you can help her, do,' she said, in a quick, broken voice; 'if you can get her out of this, for God's sake do. The police know all about it. I've split already. But her life is not safe in such a den as this. Save her if you can. Will you, old man? Do, now.'

And then, without waiting for any reply, Sophy Shotter backed upstairs again and disappeared. The vicar of Deepdunes descended into the shop in a state of great perplexity of mind. Here was a woman in danger, here was foul play, and he, with more knowledge of butterflies than of human nature, was scarcely strong enough for the defence. In the shop he found the thick-set, truculent Mr. Shotter waiting for him. From a pair of beady black eyes he looked out furtively at Mr. Ledwitch. His manner had completely changed. There was a new suavity of demeanour about him that was startling.

'Is she comfor'ble now?' he asked, vainly endeavouring to give a ring of sympathy to the huskiest of voices.

'I hope so.'

'The doctor doesn't think she'll pull through, poor dear. But she's young. What do you think, Mr. Mandeville?'

'She's very ill.'

'S'elp me, she just is! Can't think how the —what the deuce is the matter with her myself,' he said. 'I've pampered her jest as if she wos my own child; but she gives up somehow. Temper perhaps,' he added thoughtfully.

'I will call to-morrow again.'

'Thankee. She'll be reasonable to-morrow. She's a bit off her nut to-day—says all kinds of things, doesn't she?'

'No; she has not said much.'

'Oh. You don't want to buy a fust-rate black-and-tan, I suppose?'

'No; I don't.

'Capital dog for the house. I've got a swell parrot too, Mr.—fresh as paint, from Liverpool this morning. Not a feather wrong with him.

There he is, cage and all, for four pounds.
He'll say anything.'

It was a fine parrot, and it would say anything—that was improper. For suddenly, and
without a moment's warning, it burst into the
vilest and most shocking torrent of words, and
brought the crimson blush of shame to the
cheeks of Mr. Ledwitch. It was a clever parrot,
but hardly a clergyman's parrot.

Mr. Ledwitch waved two deprecating hands
and flew through the shop door into the street.
A dreadful den, as Sophy Shotter had called it:
even 'the fowls of the air' used bad language.

Outside in the streets, where the lamps were
lighted now, there was some one loitering. Not
the policeman in plain clothes, who had grown
tired of waiting for him, and gone back to the
station-house in Camberwell New Road, but a
very tall young man, who had given way between the shoulders somewhere, and craned
forward awkwardly—who was dressed in the
height of fashion, and wore a white hat with
a black hat-band—who had goggle eyes, and
wonderfully round, and wonderfully red features,

and who, lavishly endowed by nature with an extra length and thickness of tongue, was compelled to carry part of that article upon his chin for greater convenience. So very odd a young man was he, that the Reverend Paul Ledwitch, whose nerves had been considerably shaken that evening already, gave a little spring into the air when this individual crossed the road, and took his arm in the most friendly and confidential manner.

'How is she? Is it all up?' in the thickest of accents, and with an aggravated lisp, which it is needless to repeat here in all its richness of incoherency. Camberwell was a marvellous place for character, thought the vicar; there were extraordinary people to be encountered at every turn.

'You allude to Miss Shotter?'

'Alice Shotter, oh, yes, awfully so. Did you tell her I was waiting outside?'

'I didn't know you were outside, sir. I don't know who you are now,' said Mr. Ledwitch.

'Don't you really though? You've heard enough about me, I'll lay odds,' he said. 'I've

been the cause of all the beastly bother over
there, 'pon my soul I have, and, 'pon my soul,
nobody can be so awfully sorry as I am.   I
didn't think—I couldn't imagine—I'm devilish
cut up all round.   If anything happens to that
girl through me—I shall—just you look here.'

And, to the amazement of Mr. Ledwitch, the
tall young man produced a very bright revolver
from his pocket.

'Just bought it.   Shall send a bullet clean
through Old Shotter, and then another through
myself.'

'Good gracious, sir! put that dreadful instrument away.'

'When Shotter comes out of that shop, and is
putting up the first shutter to denote that she's
gone, I shall blaze away at him—from behind!
Do you know whom I am now?' he asked, as he
pocketed his revolver.

' You're the Bull-pup.'

'What the devil——'

'I mean you are Mr. Bullthorpe, the fourth
son of the Earl of Moo.'

'Yes, that's so.   And,' he added, in a deep

slobbering whisper, 'the most unhappy wretch
in all the world, if that poor girl dies through
me. I shall never get over it. I shall turn
monk, if I don't shoot myself, that is——which
I will. How is she?'

'Very weak.'

'I've promised her cousin not to come on the
premises, although Shotter would be glad to
see me, and to sell me something, I know; and
I've said I won't worry any more. But I can't
keep away. I'm going out of my mind. Brandy
does not do me any good now, and I take a lot
of it, too. Oh, Lord! she was a nice girl, wasn't
she? Isn't she? What do you think?'

'I think that you have behaved very dis-
gracefully, if I know anything of the story,' said
Mr. Ledwitch, severely.

'So I have. Come and have a drink—no,
we can't have a drink in this street—liquor's
beastly. We'll have a cab, and tool down to
the club, and—no, I shall not leave the neighbourhood. You are quite right, Mr.——, I forget what name you said you were—you was
—*yours was*—but I have been a brute, a beast,

a perfect monster, as regards that girl. I would
have taken her away,' he continued, 'from that
peaceful home yonder, where all the dogs and
stinking rabbits are—by gad, sir! I would have
married her. I didn't know it at the time, but I
would have rather done that than lose her, or
that she should have come to grief like this.
And when she fired up, and told me I was a
damned villain, or something of that sort, and
fetched me the awfullest slap one side of my face
—just here—I could have knelt down and wor-
shipped that girl as my guardian angel. See?'

Mr. Ledwitch saw that this fourth son of the
Earl of Moo was very close upon being a gib-
bering lunatic—that was the most palpable fact
before him at the present moment, and a very
deplorable specimen of 'softening' he was,
whether it arose from the accident of birth, or
the incident of brandy. He would be glad to
be quit of this scion of a noble house, but he did
not quite see his way to shake him off at present,
the aristocrat clutched him so tightly by the
funny-bone.

'When she got home one night there was a

row about something,' Bullthorpe went on,
'about me and some money, I think, she hadn't
borrowed, and Shotter pitched her downstairs—
awfully practical man is Shotter—and said she
shouldn't stop in his house any longer. And
altogether—but there, it is a shocking story.
I shall kill Shotter and myself, and make it
shockinger, though, if anything happens to
Alice. And, if she gets well, I mean to marry
her. Right off, straight.'

Mr. Ledwitch thought that it would be preferable for the young woman to die right off instead, but he did not express that opinion aloud.

'Do you know what I did to cheer her up
last week?—sent her a newspaper announcing
our marriage, just as it might happen, just as I
intend it shall happen, when she gets all right
again. A hint, you know; wasn't a bad idea,
was it, that I meant everything that was fair
and straight and above-board?'

'Oh, that was you?'

'Yes; a perfectly original idea, I flatter myself
it was. I put my own advertisement in the
newspaper, and slapped down some old fool's

name in it for the parson that I fished out of
the "Clergy List" at the club. Wasn't that
good feeling, Mr. ——, true repentance. Wasn't
that smart?'

'Much too smart,' said the old fool out of the
'Clergy List,' 'and risky. What did your father
say?'

'Oh, there was a row when he found it out,'
replied the Hon. Septimus Bullthorpe. 'He
thought I was married at first, and then, when I
explained how matters stood, he swore he'd
shut me up in an asylum. He wouldn't stand
any more of it.'

'Has he had much of it?' was the quiet inquiry of his clerical companion.

'Poor old man—I've been a bit wildish, I'm
afraid,' he confessed. 'But to talk of shutting
me up in a lunatic asylum, when I've got the
brains of the whole family, is rich! Well, here's
a chance of settling down, and everything
proper, and the pater ought to be glad of it.
And Alice would be a credit to anybody; she's
been well brought up—or she has brought herself up well—and she is as good as gold. She

hasn't got an uncle that is all that could be wished,' he added, thoughtfully, ' and her cousin Sophy's a scorcher; but I shall pension them off, or—or poison them. Don't quite know what to do yet. It's difficult, don't you see, to know what to do with all of them.'

'Ahem. Yes.'

' Where are you going now?'

'I'm going to find Mr. Mandeville, and——'

' Aren't you Mr. Mandeville?'

' No, I am not.'

' Oh! I thought you were the parson she makes such a fuss about, who's got a shop—I mean a church, or something—at the end of the next street. He's only a beggarly curate, you know, and is taking care of the shop—the church, I mean—for the rector, who's gone to Jerusalem with Cook's last batch.'

' Oh! indeed.'

' I shan't go any further with you, I shall wait about here till Soph sends down to tell me how Alice is. I have the pleasure,' he said, raising his hat some distance from his head, ' to wish you a good evening.'

'Good evening, Mr. Bullthorpe.'

And the Vicar of Deepdunes parted from him with alacrity. The next hour or two were spent in finding out Mr. Mandeville and Dr. Dolby, and in hearing from the former full particulars of the antecedents of Alice Shotter. Mr. Mandeville had only just returned from the country —which accounted for his not calling at Tiger House when sent for that day—and he heard the story of her present weak condition with grave interest. He was a black-haired, black-bearded young man, with a big forehead all bumps.

'She was one of the best girls in Camberwell,' he said. 'There wasn't a girl like her in the parish, in fact; and then the family got very poor, and she was forced to help them. I was afraid her taking to the music-halls was to be the end of a good young life, and I said so. I tried to stop it, I was angry, I was heart-bro——, I was rather hard, perhaps, but I didn't like it at all.'

Mr. Ledwitch went in search of the doctor after this. He found that Dr. Dolby was of opinion that there had been nearly murder done, but he kept that opinion to himself. It was not pleasant or safe, whilst attending a patient, to have that patient's father thirsting for one's blood. But he could assure Mr. Ledwitch that Mr. Shotter was one of the most desperate characters in the neighbourhood, and that the wretch had not heard the last of it.

Neither had a great many more folk. Miss Alice Shotter was worse the next day, and the police, on the evidence of her cousin Sophy, suddenly made a raid upon Tiger House, and by the aid of six of the best men in the force, and a good, strong, serviceable stretcher, conveyed Mr. Shotter to the station house. And, before Mr. Shotter came out for good, Alice Shotter was far away from his clutches—being nursed back to health and strength by a motherly old cottager near the sea-coast of Lincolnshire, whilst her cousin Sophy took charge of the business till father was free. That was Mr. Ledwitch's idea—the poor girl was better out of the way, he thought, for a while. Better out of the way, even of the Honourable Septimus

Bullthorpe, before the young man softened much more, and became dangerous. He had asked her opinion first though—lest, after all, she should be fond of the gentleman, and lose a chance of being connected with the peerage—and she said, 'Yes, she would be very glad to get away from him.'

And, having got completely out of his way, the Honourable Septimus Bullthorpe went back to the 'Pav.' and the 'Troc.' and other halls of harmony, and did marry, after all, Patty Chesterton, the 'great Variety artiste,' and was disinherited on the spot by his father the Earl of Moo—a nobleman who never stood any nonsense, and was afflicted by three more sons, all very much of the same pattern as Septimus, but not half so impulsive or warm-hearted. Sophy Shotter accepted an engagement in the States the day before her father was out of his time. It was hardly worth while waiting at home to receive his greeting, she thought. She sent a letter to Alice before her departure.

'I shan't come and bid you good-bye,' she wrote. 'You'll get on all right now, and with-

out me.   I'm more harm than good to anybody,
and that's the truth.   I'm off with the Ganderson trio, and the Chicky family.   Three pounds
a week, and all found; but Pol Ganderson is
too high and mighty for me, so there'll be a row
soon.   I'm not half so yellow as I was, thank
the Lord.   So no more at present, from your
affectionate cousin.'

There was a postscript.

'Mr. Mandeville's coming to see you by
Saturday's excursion, he says.   He ain't so bad
a sort, is he?'

And Mr. Mandeville did run down into
Lincolnshire.   And Mr. Ledwitch has a very
shrewd suspicion now—although his mother-in-
law, Mrs. Goodfields, will not believe it for an
instant—that he shall officiate at Alice Shotter's
wedding, after all; for Mr. Mandeville keeps
on running down at every available opportunity, and Alice Shotter seems very glad to
see him.

GIGSON'S GOOSE CLUB.

GIGSON'S GOOSE CLUB.

I HAVE never been quite able to make out why it has been my lot in life to have been more unlucky than most fellows of my acquaintance —to have had longer spells of bad luck, to have had luck dead against me from the beginning to the end, to have never known what it was to have a fair, fat, downright slice of good fortune handed over as my share. I cannot make it out. I never shall. I puzzle over it sometimes in my retirement from society's rude glare, for I am not above confessing that I am an indoor resident of Saint Malthus's workhouse, and have settled like a butterfly on the parish for good, by way of compensation for its 'settling' me

with its rates and taxes, summonses and distraints, when I was a respectable householder
trying as hard as I could to pay my way, and
never quite succeeding; always being just a
little behind, you know, and never able to
catch up.   That is not uncommon, is it?   I hear
that even the upper circles have the same complaint at times—but that is all hearsay, of
course.   I do not know anything about them.   I
do not want.

What I should like to know, in these latter
days, struggling with underdone gruel, contract
bread, and bits of gristle which would wreck
the stoutest gums, is why I have never got on
in life, or never had the chance of getting on?
I have asked the question of myself, I have put
the question to my friends, and from my friends
I have had lots of answers, guesses at the
enigma, candid explanations—'straight tips,' as
they politely call them, when they wish to say
anything extra cutting,—but they are wide of
the truth, all of them.   Everybody is wrong.
There is a deeper reason for it than it has been
in their power to fathom; the mystery, the

hard luck, and the cruel injustice of it remain inscrutable.

I have been told that I was always 'too easy,' as if being too easy, even if it were true—should be a crime to be visited by the sentence of the Union; that I did not attend to business —which is a libel; that I was too fond of political argument in the bar-parlour of the 'Regent,'—as if political argument were not the glorious prerogative of a free-born citizen of this mighty empire; that I was too fond of my glass, and, worse crime still, of letting other people dip into it at my expense; that I was a bit of a fool, and never knew how to take care of myself.

Well, I was generous and conversational, and unselfish and social, and this is the world's verdict. This is what people say of *me!*

But I am not writing my life and adventures; I *may* be a bit of a fool, but I am wise enough to know nobody wants a long history of how a man went down in the world. That is common enough, anyhow. This is an incident in my life—an episode, a something peculiar that hap-

pened to me before I took to the workhouse,
and scraped roads, and broke stones, and perhaps the reader will get some amusement out of
it—more amusement than I did. For there are
heaps of people to laugh at other people's
troubles—lor, how they do roar occasionally!

It was at a time when I was not particularly
prosperous. I was nearly at the bottom of the
hill, but not quite. Being of a more sanguine
disposition than Mrs. Brownash, I had had an
idea that things would take a turn. The gas
had been cut off, and we were burning oil
lamps in our little milk shop, and our regular
customers were complaining of the general
skimminess of the fluid in which we dealt, and
the water-rate was positively insulting to us
after his fourth application, and coals and
meat were 'awful dear.'

Still I was genial and hospitable to the last:
I had a cheery way with me at the worst of
times; I was the sunshine of No. 4, Birchester
Buildings; Mrs. Brownash was the ominous
cloud. She had a bad habit of prophesying
disaster, which was aggravating, especially

when it came true. I lived for the day, she
told me, poor thing. Well, that was quite
enough for me, twenty-four hours of it.

'If you weren't so much at the " Regent,"' she
would say to me, as if I could stay at home all
the evening in the beastly back-parlour and see
her darn socks till supper time. There was
nothing more monotonous; besides, after a hard
day's work, a man requires society, not socks!

I will own that I was fond of society, even the
society of my wife's relations, and that is saying
a great deal. For my wife was not fond of mine
—'couldn't abide them,' she owned frankly.
Well, they were not up to much. They never
lent me a penny, or stood security, or backed
a little bill for form's sake, but neither did her
relations for the matter of that. I was an individual who did not appear to inspire any great
degree of confidence or love in the bosom of
my kinsmen. And yet I would have done a lot
for them had the chance ever presented itself.
I had the best intentions towards them all, I
bore no one malice, I've stood scores of them,
the thirsty ones, no end of drinks. When I was

hard up, when I did not quite see my way, for all my sanguine forecast of the future when the frost should break, and I could get at the pump more freely, I even had the courage and the generosity to ask eight of my wife's relations to dinner on Christmas Day. And Mrs. Brownash was not grateful or thankful for my liberal offer to her own flesh and blood. She had, I regret to say here, reached that peculiar stage of temperament when a woman is not grateful for anything, when she's snappish and nagging, and lets you have it at every turn.

'What have you asked them all to dinner for?' she rasped out, when I told her the news.

'I thought *you* would be pleased to have them about you,' I said, with emphasis; 'your own kith and kin.'

'Perhaps I should if there was anything to give them to eat,' she murmured, in a low voice.

'There will be plenty to give them to eat, Sarah,' I said.

'How's that?'

'Didn't I tell you I was in Gigson's Goose Club?'

'You are !'

'Yes,' I said.

'You don't mean in a raffle for a goose?' she inquired, doubtfully.

'Oh! no. I have been paying a little a week from last September, Sarah, and I'm to have a splendid goose on Christmas Eve. We're all of us to have splendid geese.'

'Who's all of us?' she asked, with lack-lustre interest. I gave her the list of a few of the neighbours whom I was accustomed to meet at the 'Regent'—pleasant, amiable, jolly fellows every one of them, a little too jolly just a few of them—did not know when to stop, and all that sort of thing, one or two of them—but men of delicate feelings, keen susceptibilities, thorough knowledge of the world, deep insight into human nature, red-hot politicians of both Liberal and Conservative tendencies, honourable, upright, convivial friends, whom I greatly respected, and who cheered my solitary path in life after my milk-walk all day. My wife sniffed at their names contemptuously, but I was used to that.

'They've set you an example, such as it is. But oh! the drink you'll all get through on deposit nights. We shall have a Christmas dinner I suppose for once, if you keep up your payments,' she added.

'If!' I exclaimed.

And I did keep up my payments—the landlord of the 'Regent' saw to that. A keen man of business was Gigson—not a bad fellow in some respects, but with no faith in his fellow-creatures. There came a time when he even mistrusted me—that is when he could not trust me to the mean extent of half-a-quartern. But I was out of collar then, and the brokers were in. That was after Christmas—after the excitement of the event which I have sat down to narrate in the best English at my command. For I was brought up well. I married beneath me. Mrs. Brownash's education had been neglected, and she was not altogether a fit companion for me. People have been foolish enough to say, 'It's a good job you've got a sensible wife to look after you, Brownash'—but they never understood me. They thought I wanted looking

after, the idiots! I suppose they considered it
sensible of Mrs. Brownash to come stalking
into the 'Regent' at eleven P.M., or a little
after eleven sometimes, put her head round the
door and call into the parlour, 'Are you ready,
Mr. B.?' I think, to this day, that *that* was an
unfair and unladylike proceeding. That it was
lowering to me. I do not assert that I was the
only one called for, as a rule, but that makes it
none the less humiliating. However, poor
Sarah is dead and gone; I cast no aspersions
upon her; she was as deficient in tenderness as
she thought Gigson's goose would be when I got
it, and, though she had not sympathy with my
numerous misfortunes, she was not a bad wife
take her in the lump. 'A precious sight better
than such an old soaker deserved,' my wife's
sister Maria has said more than once, and to my
face too. Gord knows what she has said behind
my back. I have reason to believe that I could
have got her two years for libel at any time,
had I been so disposed. But I am of an easy,
forgiving disposition, I have intimated. A fly
might trample on me without my raising a hand

in self-defence. And yet I *have* been roused—
terribly roused—as natures like mine are prone
to be under exceptional circumstances. I was
roused at Gigson's goose time, and to some
purpose. That is the story which I am coming
to.

The goose club reached a satisfactory termination in its way. We were not all satisfied—
that goes without telling. You cannot satisfy
everybody. Gigson did not expect to do so.
We all met on Christmas Eve and received our
geese; we left our wives, or our shopmen, or
our eldest sons to see to our various businesses
—those who had businesses—and we met in the
'Regent' bar-parlour and made merry, as be-
fitted the festive season, and drank each others'
healths and the landlord's health and the landlady's health, and had what the vulgar herd call
'a high old time of it,' sitting round the room
each man with a goose under his arm.

There had been a little chaff—or rather not
a little chaff—about these geese of Gigson's.
Gigson had not been absolutely fair perhaps—
or my usual ill-luck had come to me, and I had

got the worst goose of the lot. Everything had been drawn for, fair and square—Gigson said that I had no cause for grumbling. But when a man gets a very small goose—a dropsical duck kind of goose—and that goose is not a properly proportioned bird, but has in its early gosling days either broken its chest-bone or developed a compound pigeon-breast that look-ed liked a carpenter's plain concealed under a film of goose-flesh, or done something to gene-rate an abnormal disfigurement of torso, there is an excuse for protest. And good-tempered as I was, despite my wife's relations on my mind—all coming in the morning—I did my share of grumbling till I was laughed and bantered out of my disappointment. I never could bear malice after my fifth glass of Scotch, with lemon. After that, Gigson might have palmed on me a deformed cock sparrow, and received my blessing for it into the bargain.

We were more than customarily festive that Christmas Eve; I remember that we were abso-lutely hilarious. Gigson grew grave about a quarter to twelve—when he had pocketed all our

money—and told us we were a ' sight too noisy,'
and that we had better get home with our geese
before the police stepped in and interfered.
And, after all, we were only brimming with
good fellowship. I was a trifle more brimming
than the rest, and slopped over a bit more, but
then I have told you that I was naturally of a
genial disposition, and on special occasions disposed to ' let myself go.'

I mention this to account for what follows,
when we were all outside the ' Regent' laughing and chatting in the cool night air, Slowfire,
the cheesemonger, resting his forehead against
the lamp-post because the night was not quite
cool enough for *him*. And it was not a cool night
for Christmas time, but damp, and muggy, and
foggy, and altogether disagreeable.

I do not think I have explained very clearly
where the ' Regent' was—if I say in the suburbs,
Peckham way, that will be sufficient for the
purposes of my story. The ' Regent' was at the
corner of Crayfish Street, which ran into Gumford Road, which ran into Birchester Buildings,
which ended in a brick wall and no thorough-

fare. I lived in Birchester Buildings, and my boon companions—Slowfire excepted, who thought he should feel better if he remained where he was for half-an-hour—were unanimous in their intentions to see me home—to wish me a final merry Christmas on my own doorstep— to offer Mrs. Brownash, if she would kindly accept them at so late an hour of the evening, or the early morning, all the compliments of the season.

So we marched along three abreast, keeping to the pavement because it was foggy, very foggy, and we did not wish to lose our way or be run over. We sang, 'For he's a jolly good fellow,' and other patriotic songs on our homeward journey. We roused a little too inconsiderately the echoes of the night, and set a few dogs barking, and brought Sawkins the policeman down upon us with a threat to run 'the blooming lot' of us in, until Sawkins discovered that I was one of the party, when he changed his note and his peremptory officiousness, pretty quick.

I do not think I have mentioned that Sawkins

was a second cousin of my wife's, and an active member of the metropolitan constabulary. He and I differed in politics, and on religious topics, and on the chief burning questions of the day, and did not get on very nicely as a rule, but as he lived in Birchester Buildings too, and was a relation—a very poor relation—of my wife's, and as he and his gawky girl Araminta were coming to-morrow to dinner—have I mentioned that Sawkins was a widower?—it would not have been quite in keeping with the etiquette of the position to run me in on the day of the banquet, and turn the key on the giver of the feast. He knew that as well as anybody, so begging us to go along more quietly, and muttering something about the inspector coming up the next street, he got out of our way as soon as he possibly could. I do not think Sawkins could have done less than that.

But, when we were in Gumford Road, we forgot all about Sawkins again—and the fog was so thick we were not quite certain that we were in Gumford Road at all—and Timkins began to sing again, until in a playful vein—the play-fullest manner you could conceive—Jones, always as full of humour as ever he could stick, whirled his goose round and round by the neck, and brought it down with a good honest 'bash' upon the crown of the white hat which Timkins was wearing on the back of his head.

To this day I have never been clearly able to account for Timkins losing his temper in so unseemly, sudden, and uncalled for a way. We had been full of good fellowship and harmless fun until that particular moment, nothing had gone wrong, and we were returning to the peaceful bosoms of our families with our Christmas dinners under our arms—looking forward as it were to the bright to-morrow—when Timkins, after struggling from under his hat and getting his face well out of it, spluttered forth,

' Who—who the devil did that?'

Nobody said it was Jones—nobody wanted to make words as a wind-up to a pleasant and sociable evening—and he never dreamed it *was* Jones, who was one of a three-a-breast party, much lower down in our procession. Did I say there were exactly twenty-one of us? Slowfire

would have made twenty-two, had he left the
lamp-post and come on. Jones had slipped back
to his place very adroitly, and when Timkins
twisted himself indignantly round, there was I
immediately behind him, grinning, as he said
afterwards, from ear to ear.

'That's like your stupid drunken foolery,
Brownash,' he bawled; and then, before I expected it, there came *his* goose,—a fine, fat,
fourteen pound goose of which anyone might
be proud—slap across my mouth. He might as
well have struck me with a bludgeon, for being
at the same time taken off my guard, and on
the extreme edge of the kerb, down I went into
the roadway, dragging my two friends with me,
one of whom had come in for the rest of the
blow which my features were not large enough
to accommodate. That was Simcox the shoe-
maker, who was naturally a hasty man, and at
whose precipitate action in consequence I was
not as surprised as I had been in the case of
Timkins. For, before I could avenge my own
wrongs at this unfair and cowardly assault,
Simcox had sprung to his feet and run at

Timkins, and overturned him—unfortunately on to me, just as I was getting up and putting myself straight.

I remember very little more except that there was a general *mélée* after this, a taking of sides as friendship or chance directed, a deal of bad language and brute force, a scuffling and budging of each other into various front gardens, and then out again into the middle of the road, a banging of each other's heads with goose-flesh, combined with much shouting and a general mix up. I am sure blows were freely interchanged, and that I received more than my fair share of them—that I felt at last I was fighting for my life,—and that people from their upstairs windows were screaming 'fire' and 'murder.'

I became conscious at last that the battle was over, and that we were all shaking hands again, and apologising one to another, and saying it was all fun, and weeping on one another's shoulders, and wondering how it had all happened that we should have suddenly thirsted as it were for each other's blood, and made

such awful idiots of ourselves. And I had
dropped my goose in the confusion somewhere
—and there was not a trace of it left—not a
sign of it anywhere. That was the extraordinary mystery of it all. The goose had vanished
utterly and completely. Here were twenty-
one of us, and only twenty geese. The hump-
chested bird was no longer of my world.

We stood in a compact little mob, and considered the position. I received the sincere
condolences of all my friends—even Timkins
condoled with me, as I had forgiven Timkins'
unjustifiable onslaught—and every man Jack
offered to be searched from top to toe if I should
have the remotest suspicion that any one of
them had got my goose.

I did not suspect them—I told them that I
would prefer death at the stake to suspecting
the most unworthy of the score of them—and
they believed me. They were sorry and
bewildered—they put themselves in my place
and were exceedingly distressed—they swore,
very improperly, not to leave me till the goose
was found—and they were indefatigable in their

search without result. We went into all the front gardens, and groped about on our hands and knees; we retraced our steps to Crayfish Street, we grovelled about the gutters, we ran against each other in the fog, we scoured the pavement on both sides of the way, we lighted all the matches and vesuvians we had in our respective pockets, but there was no light thrown on the missing goose.

It was a blow to me. A greater blow than Timkins, in the heat of the moment and with his blood boiling in his veins, had given me some time before. I was utterly overcome. I sat down on the kerbstone with my back against a letter-box and nursed my sorrow. I dared not face Mrs. Brownash alone under the peculiar circumstances of the case, and not one out of the score of them talked any more of accompanying me home to wish Mrs. B. all the compliments of the season. Oh! no—that would not do now, they were sure of it, the cowards!

Timkins said to me,

'What's the use of sitting there, Brownash?'

'I don't know.'

'You'll catch your death of cold?'

'I don't care.'

'Are you coming on?' Simcox said.

'I ain't a-coming on.'

'Then stop where you are!' was Simcox's brutal remark as he marched away from me.

After that the party broke slowly up. I daresay I was obstinate and hard to manage— and the hour *was* late, and there were other wives waiting for their husbands' return besides Mrs. Brownash. I daresay if I had had five 'Scotch's' instead of six, it would have rendered me more ductile and flexible, for I declined to move from my position, and the letter-box sheltered me from the wind, and there was only cold comfort at home.

My old companions drifted from me by degrees —most of them with their teeth chattering; the cold grew more intense, and the fog thicker. Jones was the last to go, but he too finally gave me up in despair.

'You'll be found frozen to death in the morning, and there'll be a pretty go,' said Jones, in warning accents.

'I'm quite warm enough, thank you.'

'I can't stop any longer.'

'I ain't asking you to stop, am I?'

'I shall tell the first policeman to keep an eye upon you,' he said.

'That's right; tell Sawkins.'

'Are you sitting here with any hobject, or hain't you?' Jones asked, snappishly. He was rather an ignorant fellow was Jones, though not bad company at the 'Regent.' At the 'Regent' Jones was at his best.

'Yes, I have a hobject,' I said, with considerable satirical emphasis, but he did not seem to see it.

'What is it?'

'I am not going home without my goose.'

'But you can't find it.'

'I shall when it's daylight, I daresay, and if some of you fellows haven't nicked it.'

After which ungenerous remark, Jones walked home without so much as another word. He was the last of them, and I was left alone in my glory in Gumford Road.

Very probably he did me a good turn after

all, though I did not think so when the news
came to me days and days afterwards, that he
had found out Sawkins and told him where I
was and what I was doing, and begged Sawkins
to keep an eye on 'the obstinate old beggar,'
and so Sawkins came tramping round to find me
a quarter-of-an-hour afterwards.

Have I said that Sawkins was a rough, uncultured bully of a man, and of a policeman?
I think I have implied so. There was no more
refinement in him than in a pig. I fancy I must
have dozed off a little after Jones had gone, for
I was certainly not prepared for my wife's second
cousin suddenly catching me up under the arm-
pits and propping me against the letter-box.

'Upon my soul and body, relation or no
relation, I'll run you in, Brownash, if you give a
fellow all this blessed trouble,' were the first
words he murmured--very hoarsely--in my
ears. 'What the blazes have you been sitting
here for?'

'Haven't you heard the dreadful news?'

'Yes. You've lost your goose. Well, this
isn't the way to find it, is it?'

'How would you set about it?' I asked, sarcastically.

'I wouldn't set here,' said the ungrammatical beast: 'I'd go home, and come back when it's daylight. Though,' he added, illogically, 'that's not a bit o' use.'

'Why ain't it?'

'Some of your mates has got it fast enough. It's one of their larks, you may stake your daddy on that.'

'If I thought so—I'd—I'd—I'd be the death of the thief.'

'I daresay you'll find it tied to the knocker, or sent round in the morning, or somethink,' he suggested; 'you're all a bit on, and don't know what you're about.'

'Sawkins,' I said, gravely, 'if you say another word, I'll report you to your inspector.'

This annoyed Sawkins—a crude, rough-handed jack-in-office, clad in a little brief authority. You know the kind of man I mean.

'Look'ee here, Brownash. Cheek is a thing I never did stand from a cove in liquor,' he said. 'Now, for the last time, are you a-goin' home,

or ain't you a-goin' home? Let's have it.
Straight.'

He could afford to be insolent and tyrannical
now. There was no goose for to-morrow's dinner—there was no dinner at all, for the matter of
that. It was a fine look-out, the Lord knows.
He could tower over me with his superior youth
and strength. He was only forty-two, and as
big as an ox—one of your big beasts.

'Well, I'm going home,' I said, sullenly at last.
' Will that do for you?'

' It's the wisest thing you can do,' he replied.

'I don't know that. I'd just as soon be run
in out of Mrs. Brownash's way till it blows over.
But,' I added, ' the first thing in the morning I
shall be out again. The goose is somewhere
about. The damned thing can't fly.'

'Your mates have got it,' said the positive
Sawkins again ; ' don't I keep telling you so ?'

'You're precious wise, you are,' I muttered.
Then I walked homewards, and he walked after
me, trying to keep an eye on me. I dodged
him there, though. I crossed over the way,
doubled in the fog, and left him wondering what

had become of me. I was not going to be
followed about by him—not if I knew it. But
I went home. After all, it was about the best
thing that could be done, although only Sawkins had said so.

Over the incidents of that return home I draw
a veil. The reader shall be mercifully spared
the recital of family bickerings and injustice, of
accusation and recrimination, of what Mrs.
Brownash said to me, or I said to Mrs. Brownash, and how Mrs. Brownash's sister—have I
mentioned before that I consider Mrs. Brownash's sister a spiteful old cat?—backed up Mrs.
Brownash in acrid remarks of her own, which
proved conclusively to me that she was the
most waspish being that ever was weighed in
the scale of feminine humanity. I will not
sully these pages with assertions against my
own name and fame, uttered by the bone of my
bone, the flesh of my flesh, the scrag of my
scrag.

I had no peace. I tried to laugh away the
storm, or to make head against it, or to submit
in sullen despair to it. Their conduct, their in-

sulting remarks, their stream of abuse kept on.
It was as well, I thought—I believe I told them
in plain words—that there were no children
about us now to learn how their poor mother
went on. For our Sally was married and gone
from us to Holloway. She and her husband,
and their first baby, were expected to dinner
on Christmas morning; I had sent them an invitation myself. I slept through the storm at
last—I went calmly and placidly off in the
midst of the turmoil, with my head resting on
the counter in the shop, whither I had gone to
escape their bitter personalities. I will do them
the justice to say that they did not try to wake
me till it was time to proceed on my rounds with
the milk. 'We shall get some sense out of him
when he sleeps it off,' were the last words I
heard my sister-in-law say. If ever I am up for
manslaughter, my sister-in-law will be the
defunct plaintiff for the prosecution. Sleep
what off, I wondered. What did she think I
was going to sleep off?

I woke up lateish, and with a nasty head-ache.
It had been daylight more than an hour, and at

the first streak of dawn I had promised myself to look for my goose before the hand of the despoiler should carry it away. The hour had come and gone, and so had the goose; it was too late. The fog had cleared away, and it was bright sunshine without. I went down Gumford Road with my wares. My 'Milk bee-low' was full of the most mournful cadence. I seemed to realise my loss, the disappointment of the family, and the invited guests more clearly in the morning, and with a splitting pain behind each ear. It was a dark and dreary mood of mine that day.

I need hardly say there was no sign of the goose in the neighbourhood—geese are not picked up every hour of the day in the public streets, at least not the kind of geese I am alluding to just now! There was a rackety look about the street that early morning—signs of our last night's revelry and high spirits and little amicable disputes. Twenty-one fellows all on the rampage together do leave traces behind them for an hour or two after their departure. I noticed sadly that the front

gardens of some of the houses appeared to have
been disturbed, that there was a downy fluffi-
ness on many of the shrubs, that a laurel or two
stood sideways or out of the ground, and that
the box-edging here and there had been sat
upon, and that two windows were broken at
Nos. 4 and 5 inclusive. The lamp-post looked
a little askew, too; but that must have been
fancy.

I delivered milk at No. 5—Miss Clasper's—a
vinegarish old maid who was always up so un-
conscionably early that I used to think she sat
up for the milk and then went to bed for the
day.

I gave her a merry Christmas as she took in
her 'ha'poth,' and it struck me at once that
she focussed me with a peculiar green and
swivel eye which she possessed. She had two
eyes, of course, but only one that was really
swivel.

'You're not looking well, Mr. Brownash, this
morning,' she said.

'Don't you think so, Miss Clasper?'

'Is anything the matter?'

'I have had a bad night. Couldn't sleep hardly at all,' I explained.

'Oh, good gracious!' she exclaimed, indignantly. 'Don't talk about bad nights. Of all the streets in London this is the worst, I verily believe. Of all the rows and rioting last night —here, outside my very door, and not a policeman to be seen—a set of drunken, idle wagabones that ought to be hanged, the lot of them. I wish I could only catch a few of them, the uproaring scoundrels. They broke that window of mine, and next door too—just you see, poor Mrs. Glander's, who's been in bed, down with a cold in her head, poor thing! for the last fortnight. What they were pitching about, all of them, the Lord knows. But I shall go round to the station after breakfast.'

'It might be as well.'

'The fact is, Mr. Brownash, the neighbourhood isn't what it was.'

'It isn't,' I said. 'I've seen the change coming on some time, ma'am.'

'It's a drunken neighbourhood.'

'I am almost afraid to think it is. And a

I 2

thieving neighbourhood, too, Miss Clasper.'

'If people only kept to this, like you and me,' said Miss Clasper, holding up the milk-jug.

'Ah! if they only did.'

I could not abide milk myself—without half-a-quartern of rum to take the rawness off it—but I thought it was not worth while to state this to a lady who was a staunch teetotaller and wore a blue ribbon under a medallion photograph of her mother, a worthy but ugly old lady, all cap and scowl.

'And a great thieving neighbourhood,' Miss Clasper went on—and she would always go on for hours if anyone had the patience to listen to her. 'You're right there, Mr. Brownash. Nothing is safe in these parts. Why, you see my mounting-ash with the red berries over there. I have been saving them berries to decorate my parler, as holly's so drefful dear this Christmas. Well, would you believe it that a man was up the tree—a big, hulking brute he was too—stripping it of every berry this morning. And I really believe it was a policeman,

but he got down in such a hurry when I scream-
ed to him, and went away at such a rate, and I
was that flurried, that I shouldn't like positively
to say, because——'

'A policeman—up that tree?' I said, very
thoughtfully.

'A policeman, or something.'

'What time was it, ma'am?' I asked, in a
trembling voice.

'It was just coming daylight. I couldn't sleep
after the fight, or riot, or revolution, or whatever it was going on outside, and, when I saw
a streak of daylight, I thought I'd pull my blind
up and read a bit from my poor dear old
mother's "Book of Martyrs;" and, when I saw a
man in the tree outside, you might have knocked me down with a hair-pin, and——'

'Are you sure he was after the berries?' I
asked. 'Hadn't he something in his hand—a
bird, or anything?'

'Policemen don't go birds-nesting at this time
of year,' said Miss Clasper, contemptuously,

'I don't mean a live bird. A goose—a Christmas goose—for instance.'

'Mussy on us! Your brain is a-turning, Brownash. Good-morning.'

And Miss Clasper shut the door, and, for the only time in her life, was the first to close the conversation.

I went the rest of my way, 'buried in the deepest thought,' like a villain in a penny novelette. Was Sawkins—my wife's second cousin, allied to her by blood and to me by law —the man who had climbed the mountain-ash, and had he gone up the tree after my goose? Was it not possible that in the playful exuberance of our spirits the goose—my goose—had been tossed out of my hands and hurled, as it were, into the tree, and that there it was hanging in the morning like a blossom for the rude hand of the first wayfarer to pluck? And had Sawkins been that first wayfarer? I believed he had.

When I was close at home—Sawkins lived next door but one from my 'Dairy-and-Families-waited-on-daily-Emporium'—I called at Sawkins' house. I knew he would have gone to bed to sleep off the fatigue of his

night duty—that he would be in his first sleep
even—but I did not care much about that. All
that was in my mind was the fate of the goose
I had received from Gigson's club. Had
Sawkins found it, and taken it home for me? I
wanted to be quite sure of that before I faced
Mrs. Brownash again. And it did not seem at
all unlikely that Sawkins was saving it for me,
so that I could return home with it and say to
Mrs. Brownash that it was only my fun last
night, and I had left the goose to be called for,
all the while.

I knocked at Sawkins's door. Araminta
Sawkins, his daughter, was out, which I thought
a little bit singular before eight in the morning;
and the door had been left ajar to save Sawkins
the trouble of opening it for her when she
returned. There was nobody else in the house,
and my wife's second cousin was evidently upstairs in his chamber taking his rest, perhaps
with his martial cloak—or his shiny cape—
around him. I looked about the premises,
peeped in the parlour and kitchen, looked under
the sofa and into an old meat-safe in the back-

yard; but there was no goose anywhere. Finally, I stood at the bottom of the stairs and shouted up 'Sawkins!' till I thought I should have bust myself.

Sawkins heard me at last. He was a good hard sleeper, but I was too much for him. His bed-room door was flung open, and he responded:

'Hullo, down there—wot's up? Wot's the row about?' he bawled down to me. 'Who is it?'

'It's *me*, Sawkins.'

'Who's me?'

'Brownash. Did you see anything of my goose when it was daylight, Sawkins, this morning?'

I fancied Sawkins paused before he replied:

'No, I didn't.'

'Oh.'

'I didn't think no more about your goose,' he grumbled. 'Is that all you've been and woke a feller up for?'

'All indeed. Isn't it enough?'

'Have you anything more to say to me?'

I hesitated. I thought I would tell him what Miss Clasper had seen, and hint that he had been shockingly neglectful in his duty not to see people clambering up trees and damaging property on his very beat, but I thought I would not. Have I already mentioned that I am of a peaceable and forgiving disposition? I think I have.

'Yes, Sawkins. This needn't make any difference.'

'What needn't make any difference?'

'You shall have a dinner of some kind all the same, old fellow. If it's bread and cheese and new-laid milk, it shall be something.'

'I ain't a-comin'.'

'What?'

'I've got another invitation,' he responded, gruffly. 'I'm going round to a friend. Keep your bread and cheese.'

And then Sawkins—have I indicated before that Sawkins was a rude uncultured savage?—slammed the door and went back to bed.

'You needn't come if you don't like. Nobody

wants you,' I called back, but I do not think he heard me.

I went into the front again, and left the door ajar as I had found it. I took up my milk cans, and walked out at the front gate, where I met Araminta Sawkins, without a bonnet and with five raw onions and a lot of sage in her apron.

' Been shopping, Araminta ?'

' Yes, Mr. Brownash.'

' A merry Christmas to you, Araminta.'

' Thank'ee, Mr. Brownash. And the same to you.'

' You're not coming to dinner with us after all.'

' Ain't we though ?'

' Your father has altered his mind.'

' Lor ! has he though ?'

Have I mentioned before—no, I have not mentioned before—that I always considered Araminta Sawkins a sly girl—one who could not look you in the face, and who gave you the impression that she was deceiving you with your eyes open ?

And I had my eyes open now. What did
Araminta Sawkins want with sage and onions?
What was the need for them—and in so great a
hurry—if that thief Sawkins had not got my
goose? I was quite sure he had got it. There
was circumstantial evidence enough to hang him
already. My goose at the present moment in
all probability was under Sawkins' bed or his
pillow. And yet such a man could sleep on
undisturbed.

I may have mentioned before that I was a
man of some determination when once roused
to action; and I was thoroughly roused now.

'Mrs. Brownash,' I said to her on my return,
and when I found both her and Maria putting on
their bonnets and tying the strings under their
sharp chins with most emphatic jerks, ' wherever
are you going?'

' There's your breakfast,' said my wife

' That is not a simple answer to a simple
question.'

' You're right, Brownash; it *is* a simple
question. I'm going to put the company off,
and Maria's got to get to Islington and tell my

poor gal it's no use comin' here for anythink to eat.'

'Sawkins and his girl have put themselves off already.'

'Oh! have they? I'm not sorry either. Why you ever asked Sawkins I never could make out.'

'I asked him one night when my heart was full.'

'When your skin was full, you mean,' said Maria, tartly.

'Maria,' I said solemnly, and I hope impressively, 'this is not a day, or a season, for remarks of an acid nature. You needn't put anybody off. You can off with your bonnets instead and listen to me.'

'What have *you* got to say?'

'That Sawkins has got my goose, by gord!'

'Oh! Brownash!'

'Don't mind my bad language, and think of how we are to get that goose back into the fold.'

'What do you think?'

'I have an idea.'

' You can't prove it's your goose, Brownash.'

' I would know it amongst a hundred thousand geese.   It's a hunch-back—I mean it's a narrow-chested, mal-formed animal of stunted growth.'

' And you have gone out guzzling once a week since September for that !'

' " It's a poor thing, but mine own," ' I quoted; but they did not see the application.

' It looks to me much more like Sawkins's,' said Maria ; ' but how do you know ?'

I told them the whole story, and the facts seemed singularly conclusive even to the illogical minds of Mrs. Brownash and her sister. They took off their bonnets and stood with arms akimbo considering the position. I was glad to see there was an aspect of set determination about their lower jaws which boded ill for Saw-kins. I should have auxiliary forces on my side if they were required ; and God defend the right —and the right goose !

Some hours later, at a quarter-past eleven to the minute, and after we had arranged a most complicated plan, which as it never came off need not be entered into detail here, Mrs.

Brownash saw Araminta once more leave her
father's premises and dart swiftly down the
street towards the chandler's shop at the other
corner, with a plate in her hand and her hair
streaming in the wind. Have I mentioned that
Araminta Sawkins was an untidy creature unless
dressed to death upon Bank holidays?

'Leave this to me,' said Maria.

And Mrs. Brownash and I thought at first
that we would leave it to Maria. We could
trust Maria in anything of that kind. Besides,
Maria's feelings were hurt. She was very fond
of goose.

'I'll follow her and have it out,' she said.

'And I'll have it indoors,' I said. 'I'll slip round
to Sawkins. You'd better wait a minute, Maria.'

'All right.'

Sawkins would be still in bed. I knew his
habits, and that he would not get up till twelve.
But he was an early diner, and the goose must
be cooking now and at my mercy. And if he
had my goose! The door would be left ajar
again for the return of Araminta—probably with
a dab of butter to baste the goose with.

I went cautiously but swiftly up to the front door lest Sawkins should be shaving his ugly black muzzle at the first-floor window. The door was ajar as I had anticipated. I stole into the passage : heaven ! the odour of roast goose permeated the whole establishment of Sawkins.

Yes, there it was, roasting at the back-kitchen fire, my goose, my small, chest-contracted, long-lost, subscription goose—the worst one of the whole lot; but I seemed to love it all the more on account of its infirmities and the vicissitudes which the poor thing had undergone. I could have sworn to it anywhere. I had no scruples. I was defying the law, and the strong limb of the law wallowing in his bed upstairs; but I had a goose party coming off that day, and that bird was mine.

It was but the work of an instant to unhook the goose from the bottle-jack and decamp with it, clutched, hot and steaming, to my chest. Another moment, and it was in my own house safe and sound. Villainy had met with its reward, and was completely baffled. Not a soul had seen me come out.

'It's nearly done already,' said Mrs. Brownash.

'We must backen it a bit,' remarked Maria.

'It's a miserable little bird. I never saw so small a goose in my life,' added my better half, 'and, mussy on us, look at the breast of it.'

'It's a recognisable goose. Let us be thankful for that, at any rate,' I said, severely, perhaps a little sarcastically.

And we were thankful, and our dinner-party went off very comfortably, and there was enough to go round, too, as Sawkins and his daughter had declined to join us at the last moment. They had thought to have that goose all to themselves, the greedy creatures; but Nemesis had overtaken them. Just about our dinner time, Sawkins and his daughter were standing at their front gate looking disconsolately and dismally down the street. Later on they went out for a little walk.

And to this day Sawkins does not know how he came to lose his goose, and I have not thought it worth while to say anything about it. Mrs. Brownash, who joined the Salvation Army a few months before she died of tambourine on the brain, had what she called her 'squalms' at the eleventh hour, and wondered if, after all, I had really taken my own goose back or coolly stolen Sawkins's; but I have never had a doubt of it myself, and I am more thoroughly convinced of it with every day that I live. And Sawkins will own it some day, perhaps, when his conscience pricks him a little more. Say when he becomes 'that able and intelligent officer, Inspector Sawkins,' of the Metropolitan Police Force.

SAMUEL CROCKETTY'S SHOES.

SAMUEL CROCKETTY'S SHOES.

I DO not think it would be quite fair to my uncle and aunt—any more than it would be quite fair to my great-uncle Crocketty—if I did not state by way of a beginning that there were faults on both sides. There were a great many faults on both sides, for the matter of that, although I need not particularise all of them. The most salient will appear in the course of this narrative, and when I have got used to the telling of it; for I find writing hard work, not being a professional story-teller, and having plenty to do, without wasting my time in that way, Richard says, disparagingly. But, this being a curious little story in its way, I thought

I had better put it down, if only for the sake of the moral that is in it, and I think my readers —if I am fortunate to secure any—will be able to see the moral for themselves, without my speaking of it any more.

I am the niece of Mr. and Mrs. Filkin—my poor, dear, dead and gone father was Mr. Filkin's elder brother—and I am Selina Filkin, at your service, and at the service of Uncle Filkin and his wife—a childless, crotchetty, quarrelsome couple—had I been from a gawky girl of fourteen, until my years of discretion at one and twenty, at which period my story commences, when my great-uncle Crocketty, whom I had never seen before, came to live with us for good—for ever and ever, until, as Uncle Gregory Filkin said piously and resignedly, it should please the Lord to take him, and for that event he waited, for awhile with becoming patience and fortitude.

Samuel Crocketty came to us in a very bad way indeed, and with a duly certified announcement from a medical authority of the very highest eminence, and for whose opinion the highest

fee almost upon record had been paid by Mr.
Crocketty, that Samuel would not last another
three weeks; and, with this perfect and honourable understanding as between man and man,
Uncle Filkin took him in. And he was not
backward in repeating to his wife, in hours of
retirement—and when I could hear them perfectly well through the thin partition of lath and
plaster between their room and my little six-
feet-by-eight apartment over the shop door—
that he, Gregory Filkin, had been taken in
instead—most egregiously taken in, he was
positive.

For though Samuel Crocketty never perfectly
recovered the use of his limbs, and shuffled about
in a creepy-crawly manner, and brought the
hearts into our respective mouths, several times
a day, by slipping down a stair or two or
dropping into an unseemly position on the
passage mat, upon which he would sit and smile
benignantly until assisted to rise, certain it was
that he recovered the complete use of his mental
faculties; and as fine an appetite as anyone
could possibly require came round also with his

convalescence. And though I was very pleased
to see the odd old gentleman come round—for
I had taken to him because he was so very
much alone in the world, so very old, and feeble,
and deaf, and helpless, and obstinate, poor dear
—yet I do not think Gregory Filkin was very
pleased, though I hardly like to say so in print;
or that Mrs. Filkin, Samuel Crocketty's only
daughter, too, was as greatly exhilarated by the
event as most daughters would have been under
similar circumstances.

But then Uncle Filkin and his wife were not
quite like other folk whom I had ever met or
heard about, or read of. They had had a hard,
grinding time of it in their early days, and had
become hard in return, and had even been
ground somewhat to an edge. They were sour-
tempered folk enough, but then adversity and
grim associations and surroundings will sour
people; even when they get in the sun it is too
late, and the heat only withers—not ripens—a
good many of them. At all events, it did not
ripen Uncle and Aunt Filkin; of that I am quite
certain. I set nothing down in malice by say-

ing as much as that, or by adding that they were sour and hard to me. This is partly the subject of my story, or helps to make it one.

Perhaps I took to my great-uncle-by-law Crocketty because he was the first to find this out, and to put questions to me which were embarrassing to answer, as I had to shout my replies down a cowhorn-kind of ear-trumpet, and they could be heard over the whole house. They were such very peculiar questions, too, and not warranted by the length of our acquaintance.

'Are you comfortable here?' he asked, one winter's morning, when he had taken the only easy chair in the room and planted himself in the full front of the fire, and opened his daily newspapers at the theatrical advertisements, which he always read first.

He was peering through his thick-rimmed glasses critically at me, and his dark eyes and scanty white filaments of hair seemed in strange contrast as I looked back at him. I was setting the back parlour in order after breakfast; Uncle Filkin was in the shop booking an order for a child's funeral with a becoming expression of countenance—I have not mentioned that Mr. Filkin was an undertaker in the Trumanbury Road, E.—and my aunt was upstairs and very busy too.

'Ye—es. Oh, yes,' I replied, through his trumpet.

'Happy, Selina?'

'Why should I not be happy?' I rejoined, a little evasively.

I could not tell Mr. Crocketty that I had my little troubles, or my great ones, according to one's way of looking at them, and that happiness just then was a long way round the corner of the next street.

'You don't look happy,' he affirmed, 'that's all.'

'Oh, you must not judge by appearances,' I replied, and in order to throw him off his guard I laughed lightly down his trumpet and tickled his ear, which he began vigorously to rub.

'Don't blow me, Selina,' he said, tetchily, 'I don't like it. Well?'

'Well?' I repeated.

'What was I saying? Oh, I remember,' he added; 'no, you don't look happy, Selina. You're bright enough, and sharp enough, and there's no grizzling about you, and you've always got a pretty smile handy; but you're not a bit happy. What's the matter?' And he put his trumpet into position again, in order to receive further particulars.

'Nothing's the matter.'

'Nothing?'

'Nothing more than usual.'

'Oh, that's it. Ah!'

Finding that I was not disposed to make him my father confessor, and that his son-in-law had come to the parlour door, and was looking over the wire-blind to see what all the noise was about—for Mr. Crocketty shouted out his questions as though I was hard of hearing too —he opened his paper afresh, and dived into the theatrical advertisements.

Mr. Crocketty was naturally interested in histrionic matters: he had been an actor for fifty years. At one time of his career it was on the cards that he was to be a great comedian,

and he escaped success by a mere hair's breadth,
all the experts had said more than once. He did
not become a great actor; he was always
painstaking and sound, but he was one of the
few thousands who are safe for any part, upon
whom any manager can rely, and whom any
manager can do without. He did not make
friends behind the footlights or across them;
but he was seldom out of an engagement
during his long professional career. He was
not genial; he had a bad habit of speaking his
mind; there was a spice of acerbity in him that
the young 'whipper-snappers' on the stage did
not relish; and he went home regularly to his
supper at Holloway, and was never seen at
public-house bars or shady clubs at all hours
after the last omnibus and train had gone, and
hansoms were necessary to get into the suburbs.
He had lived in the suburbs for economy's sake
until his wife had died, and his daughter had
married Filkin the undertaker; he had lived
frugally, almost parsimoniously, all his life, and
had put money by regularly year after year,
until it had amounted to a very decent sum,

which he had intended to add to till his dying day, had not a sudden collapse thrown out all his calculations.

So sudden and serious a collapse was it that, as I have already intimated, Samuel Crocketty was considered as good as decently defunct, and Mr. Filkin, of a calculating and even miserly spirit, thought it advisable to take charge of the old gentleman, and see that 'his last moments,' as he phrased it, were spent in the bosom of all the family that was left to him.

Samuel Crocketty's last moments were not, however, to be reckoned upon with that degree of certainty which an overwise physician had predicted, and it was one of the crying grievances of Mr. Crocketty's latter days that he had paid him all that money for an opinion 'that was not worth a brass farthing.' He did not leave the establishment of his son-in-law again; one wondered very much why he remained there, their tastes and pursuits being so strangely at variance with his own; but he was old, and 'did not want any more bother,' he asserted. He might as well be with the Filkins as with anybody else.

'Take care of me,' he said, a little helplessly, to his daughter, when he was first on the mend, 'and I'll take care of you, child.'

'I will,' she said, not too sympathetically; 'it's my duty.'

'I want something more than duty, Sarah; I want attention,' he replied.

'You shall have it,' she bawled down his trumpet.

'And all the theatrical papers, Saturdays and Sundays.'

'Sundays! Very well; but it's most dreadful, father.'

'And a cup of tea about six in the morning, and a glass or two of Scotch whisky going to bed,' he added.

Sarah Filkin sighed.

'I daresay I shall not bother you very long, and there's a good bit of property in the Three per Cents., tell Filkin. That'll cheer him.'

'It will.'

'That'll induce him to put up with me. For he doesn't like me, Sarah. Does he now, on your word and honour?'

'I don't think he does,' replied his truthful daughter.

'And I don't like him. You may tell him so, if you like.'

' There's no occasion, father.'

' You need not be afraid of hurting his feelings.'

' I am not.'

' Why don't you tell him, then ?'

'He knows it already,' replied Mrs. Filkin.

' Very likely.'

It was very likely. Samuel Crocketty was not an adept at disguising his feelings, and he had not taken any great pains to conceal from his son-in-law that he utterly abhorred him and his calling, and all his ways. They were opposite poles. Mr. Crocketty, I regret to add, was of the world, worldly—free and easy, and at times irreverent—and his son-in-law considered himself 'serious.' Mr. Filkin's was a serious profession certainly, but he was not as festively disposed as are most undertakers doing a good business. He went both to church and chapel; church in the morning and chapel in the evening, and his father-in-law told him frankly he was doing it for an advertisement; he took a prominent part in the parish; he was a vestry-man, and made speeches at the town-hall; he was fond of writing letters to the local journals; he was the owner of four small houses in a rookery called Chunk Street, at the back of his own establishment, and collected his own rents, and was so hard on the tenants if they got into arrears that it was considered not at all im-probable one of these fine days that he would return home from his collection with his throat cut, or his skull stove in, both those operations having been threatened him with alarming frequency of late days, the late days being the winter time, when Mr. Crocketty was better, and taking up too much room before the fire, and altogether somewhat in the way.

'How I should like to bury that man!' I heard Mr. Filkin say in the middle of the night, quite savagely.

'Hush! Selina will hear you,' said my aunt.

'I don't care if she does,' he growled, 'I

can't stand him.   I must chuck him up : I must,
indeed.   He's too much for anybody.'

'We must all have our trials, Gregory,' she
replied,' 'and papa is a great age.'

I shivered at my aunt's placidity, and then I
felt all of a glow with indignation.

'I don't believe he's as old as he says he is?'
asserted Mr. Filkin.

'It's down in the family Bible, dear.'

'Drat your family Bible,' was the profane
remark, which assured me, if I had not had my
doubts before, that Gregory Filkin was far
from being as serious as he had led people, who
did not know him any better, to imagine.

My uncle, however, was civil enough to the
face of his father-in-law, though his obsequious-
ness did not in any way tend to impress the
old gentleman.   He was more civil when it
oozed out by slow degrees that Samuel
Crocketty had saved the respectable sum of
twenty thousand pounds.   He had not anticipated Mr. Crocketty being worth so much as that,
and, although in his heart of hearts he did not
believe that his father-in-law had come by the

amount honestly, Filkin was supremely glad to hear that it was lying in his father-in-law's name in the Bank of England. It gave a fresh zest to life and business.

'I hope you've made a will, sir?' he said, on the day Samuel Crocketty had become so strangely confidential.

'No, I haven't.'

'Ah! that's not wise of you; for, although you may live for years and years, you may be taken off at any moment, Mr. Crocketty.'

'Well, what of it?' asked the old man, sharply. 'You and Selina will come into all the money, won't you?'

'There'll be no end of money to pay for letters of administration—extra expenses right and left—extra worry.'

'Yes, it will be a trifle more expensive for you,' said Mr. Crocketty, with a chuckle; 'but you must not mind that.'

'Oh, but I do mind it,' said Mr. Filkin, losing his self-command for once as he poured forth his eloquence into the ear-trumpet of his father-in-law. 'It's the duty of every person to make

a will. It's cowardly, it's selfish to evade
it.'

'So it is.'

Mr. Crocketty was silent and thoughtful the
rest of the evening. The next day he was
very busy with pen, ink, and paper for half-an-
hour.

'I've made my will,' he said, at dinner-time;
'it only wants signing and attesting by people
not pecuniarily interested in the contents.'

'Selina and Bloggs, the apprentice, shall
witness it,' said my uncle.

'Selina must not witness it. I have left her
five hundred pounds.'

'Good gracious!' said my uncle; 'you—you
might have trusted Selina's future to us.'

'We have no children,' said my aunt. 'She
will have all that we have, when it pleases the
Lor——'

'Yes—yes; I hope she will,' interrupted my
uncle; 'but it may not please the Lord to get
rid of the two of you for ever so long, and a
little ready-money is always handy to a young
woman alone in the world. Encourages the

young fellows to come forward, eh, Selina?' he said to me, quite jocosely.

'Don't jest, father,' reproved his daughter. 'This is a solemn duty you have undertaken——'

'A legacy duty,' he added.

'And the sooner it is signed and sealed and off your mind, the better' she concluded.

'It don't want any sealing; and it isn't on my mind,' he remarked.

It was a short will. He was not averse to any one of the family knowing its contents, which were embodied in a very few lines. It bequeathed me five hundred pounds, and, after that payment, all that he died possessed of went to his dear daughter Sarah Filkin, of Trumanbury Road, E. Mr. Crocketty signed this document with a firmer hand than usual, and two young men—Bloggs, the apprentice, and his brother, who had been tap—tap—tapping at coffin nails in the back premises all the morning—were called to bear witness to the signature, which they did with their mouths full of nails.

'I hope they're satisfied now,' Mr. Crocketty said to me later on. 'They've been worrying me long enough,'

There was a peculiar look on his face that struck me as I looked at it. One could almost imagine he was bursting with suppressed laughter at something.

'Are you alluding to the will?'

'Yes, I am. You haven't thanked me for putting your name in it, Selina.'

'Thank you very much, sir,' I replied, down the trumpet; 'but I didn't expect it, and I hope I shan't have the money for many, many years.'

'You really mean that?'

'I do, indeed, sir,' I answered, warmly; 'and I hope you believe me.'

He looked hard at me for awhile.

'Yes, I do believe you,' he said, after a long stare that had become very embarrassing to me; 'and that's more than I should have believed of my daughter or Filkin, had either said as much to me. But I wanted peace, and I have nowhere to go, and this place is handy for my

funeral, and Filkin can do it trade price, the—
the vagabond.'

'Mr. Crocketty!'

'Oh, well, I don't like Filkin,' he said, shaking his head; 'I shall never like Filkin.'

'I'm sorry.'

'Are you so fond of him yourself, Selina?'

'He's my father's own brother,' I replied, as if
that were answer sufficient.

'Does he not object to young Richardson, the
grocer?'

'Oh good gracious! Who told you about Mr.
Richardson?'

'I have seen Richardson hanging about the
premises,' he replied; 'and I know Filkin
objects to him, and wants you to marry the old
pawnbroker over the way. Isn't that true?'

'Quite true,' I confessed.

'Well, don't marry the pawnbroker, for all his
diamonds, second-hand watches, and flat-irons.
Young Richardson is not in luck's way, and
there's a big opposition to him next door but
one; but my five hundred pounds will come in
handy when——'

'Don't say it, sir,' I entreated; 'you are not going to die yet.'

'No, I am not,' he affirmed; 'but Filkin wants me to die—would dance for joy if he were sure I should die before the week was out; lays traps for me—death traps. And I don't think my own child is much better. Good God, think of it—my own child!' He bowed his head and hunched his shoulders, and shook with grief and indignation, till I ventured to remonstrate against the unworthy suspicions which he had. He looked up sharply at me then, a vigilant, dry-eyed man. 'You must watch for me, Selina,' he said, positively, 'and make sure that it is all fair play—that there is no under-handed business, no plotting, no damnable double-dealing to shuffle me out of the world.'

'Oh! what dreadful thoughts you have, sir.'

'I have seen so much plotting on the stage, and so many villains, and all that,' he said, half apologetically, at last. 'I have poisoned and assassinated so many people in my time—a whole army, I daresay—that I don't settle down quite to everyday life. And Filkin's a good make-up—just the character, isn't he, for a melodrama? Keep your eye on him. A comic kind of villain, but he'll do. It's a good part. It'll fetch 'em.'

He began to ramble in his speech, I thought, as he sat and looked at the red coals, with his ear-trumpet in his hands, as if he were going to stir the fire with it, and I stole away, and left him rambling in his speech. He was quite cheerful the next day, and seemed to have forgotten all his suspicions of the preceding evening: but they remained with me. They rankled within me, kept me watchful, made me distrustful of my kith and kin, led me to see motives and designs in the most commonplace of words and deeds, rendered me nervous and unhappy.

And then that terribly thin wall between the Filkins and myself, like a compound scene in one of the melodramas of which the old actor had spoken, and the awful moments when they forgot my proximity, and *would* talk indiscreetly—would count the hours of Samuel Crocketty's life, and wonder how long he would last, and when the signs would show themselves more clearly of his breaking-up for good. This waiting for the dead man's shoes—the shoes of Samuel Crocketty—horrified and saddened me, set me in an unreal world, and made of me a watcher in spite of myself. Shall I confess that there seemed so slight a line drawn between the wish that he should die, and the darker wish to help him on his road? ·

About Christmas time Mr. Crocketty caught a severe cold. He had gone for a long walk ; his umbrella had been mislaid—was not to be found anywhere—and to lose his umbrella was inevitably to throw him into a fit of passion that was extremely reprehensible and dangerous. Uncle Filkin offered him his own, a very dingy gingham, like a chaise umbrella cut down and grown baggy, in exchange for Mr. Crocketty's own slim, dapper silk, and the old gentleman declined it, and toddled down the street in high dudgeon.

'I don't think it will rain,' Mr. Filkin called after him, 'and——'

'I don't care a damn if it does,' Mr. Crocketty called back as they separated.

But it did rain presently, 'heavens hard,' as Mr. Filkin phrased it, and Samuel Crocketty came back wet through, out of sheer obstinacy, Mrs. Filkin said, and had a bad cold the next day.

And before the next day—indeed, before Mr. Crocketty came home from his unfortunate walk —I was as shocked as though I had seen a ' dagger and bowl' drawn forth, when I came suddenly upon my uncle taking Mr. Crocketty's umbrella from the inside of a coffin in the shop and putting it back in its usual corner.

He saw me and looked scared.

'Somebody's been playing a mean trick with Mr. Crocketty,' he said, the instant afterwards; ' why, here's the umbrella amongst the goods, Selina. I hope you haven't been hiding it on purpose. You would never do such a thing as that, I trust.'

'I!'

'You don't like him; he's aggravating; but you should treat him with a little deference and respect. After all, Selina, he's your aunt's only father, and we must bear with him,' he said. 'Put the umbrella back in its place, do.'

I did so, and I know that for a day or two Mr. Crocketty was under the impression that I had been seen in possession of his umbrella a few minutes after he had quitted the establishment in a tantrum. Uncle Filkin had seen me with it in my hand, laughing very much about something, it had been reported, and Mr. Crocketty was hardly strong-minded enough to exonerate me from suspicion, being naturally a suspicious man himself. I was young and frivolous, he thought, and for a few days, and whilst his cold lasted, he did not regard me with any high degree of favour. I did not explain. I did not feel called upon to explain. There was no specific charge, and I should not have cared to have had one made against me. Very likely in my unsettled state I might have gone away for good, and married Mr. Richardson prematurely, and before he was quite sure he should be able to keep the brokers out next quarter.

But Mr. Crocketty changed suddenly to his old demeanour—to a new, strange kindness even, as though he would make amends for any hard thoughts which he might have had of me.

This was when his cold had got worse, and the doctor had once more to be sent for. I had been standing in his bed-room, with some sheets which my Aunt Filkin had given me to place upon his bed, whilst he sat heaped under a pile of blankets in an arm-chair by the fire during the process.

I remember that night very well. It was a day or two before Christmas—a miserable night, wet and stormy without. I did not know that he was watching me attentively from over his blanket and wraps, his dark eyes glinting at me beneath his shaggy white brows. I was standing by the fire, too, with the sheets in my hand, very deep in thought—deep in an awful thought, which had made my hair feel as though it would rise on end with horror, there were such strange tinglings at the roots.

'What's the matter, Selina?' he inquired, so suddenly and sharply that I jumped again.

'Nothing,' I responded.

'What are you looking like *that* for?'

'What am I looking like what for?' I rejoined.

'You're as white as a ghost.'

'Perhaps I don't feel very well.'

'You'll have those sheets on fire, if you hold them so close to the bars,' he remarked; 'are they not dry?'

'I don't think they are quite,' I replied, 'I don't know. I think there must be some mistake.'

Then I hurried from the room, and what I said to Aunt Filkin and to Uncle Filkin—who told me I was impertinent and ungrateful, and an unsatisfactory spitfire—I do not know. I only remember that I was excited and beside myself, and said hard things to them both, and hinted at foul play, or gross ignorance, or carelessness.

When I went upstairs to Mr. Crocketty's room again, he had apparently fallen asleep in his chair. I had to rouse him, and he woke up, or seemed to wake up, with a start.

'Those are not the same sheets, Selina,' he
said.

'I have changed them. The others felt damp
to me,' I explained. 'It was only my fancy;
but I am a little nervous this evening, Mr.
Crocketty.'

'You are. And watchful, Selina—very.'

'Watchful?'

'Just what you promised that you would be.
Good girl. It's necessary.'

'No, no; I don't think that. I hope——'

He beckoned me to put my head down close
to his mouth.

'They're a bad lot—an unprincipled, heart-
less, selfish, greedy lot,' he croaked hoarsely in
my ear; 'but they won't get the better of me.'

'They are a little careless, that's all, I hope.'

'Tell your uncle and your aunt that I want to
see them both very particularly the first thing in
the morning, will you, Selina?' he said.

'Yes. But you will not say anything to
them or tell them you suspect anything or
anybody?'

'Oh, no,' he replied, almost with a chuckle.

'I have only a little news for them, that's all.'

In the morning my uncle and aunt went up-stairs to his bed-side, as if to hear a last dying speech and confession, fully prepared to receive his final blessing and have done with him. They were sure he must be very bad at last to send for them in this haste. To their astonishment, however, Samuel Crocketty was evidently much better that morning. He was sitting up in bed, picturesquely attired in a highly ornate dressing-gown—an old stage property costume, all crimson and fur, which he had utilised for everyday wear—and was eating buttered toast with evident relish.

'You'll be glad to hear I'm a new man this morning,' was his first salutation.

'We are,' said Mr. Filkin, for self and wife. 'Of course we are.'

'I caught a dreadful cold on the day you—somebody—hid my umbrella, Filkin,' he said; 'and you told me it didn't matter and it couldn't possibly rain, as the glass was so high, and then it came down cats and dogs. But I've pulled through wonderfully.'

'That is good hearing,' muttered Mr. Filkin.

'I was worried that day with business, and worry upsets a man sooner than anything else. I went to the Bank of England to sell out,' he explained.

'To sell out!' gasped husband and wife together.

'Yes; all my stock,' was the cool reply. 'Twenty thousand pounds there was of it. I think I told you this before.'

'Great heavens! Good gracious! Yes, you did,' exclaimed Mr. Filkin. 'And whatever have you done with it?'

'*I have bought myself an annuity.*'

'What!'

'I have sunk it all in an annuity to keep myself nice and comfortable for the remainder of my days,' he explained. 'I am to have two thousand five hundred a year as long as I live. And it's more than I shall want, I'm sure. I shall be able to save something out of it if I am careful and live long enough—if you take care of me, and try to keep me alive.'

'An annuity, at your age!' gasped Mr. Filkin.

'Yes, that's it.'

'Didn't you think of your family—of me and Mrs. Filkin—before you went and did such a ras——, such a selfish, such an awfully selfish thing?' cried Filkin.

'It's a capital spec,' said Mr. Crocketty, munching at his toast; 'I'm a long liver. My father did not die till ninety-three, and I'm only seventy, you know.'

'It *is* a spec; you're right,' responded Mr. Filkin, with a groan; 'and you mayn't live another twelve months.'

'Oh, yes; I shall.'

'This is a trial, father, heaven knows!' murmured his pious daughter.

'It's two thousand five hundred a year,' said Mr. Crocketty. 'It's a princely income; I shan't spend half of it.'

'Great heavens, I should think you wouldn't!' said Filkin.

'I shall start my carriage.'

'Go it, sir, go it. Start a coach and four while you are about it,' said his son-in-law, fretfully, 'and let me sit behind and blow an infernal post-horn.'

Uncle Filkin was possessed of a bad temper, which it was difficult to control, and this was in the first flush of a disappointment which it was beyond his power to disguise. He had made so sure that Samuel Crocketty's shoes would be stepped into with ease and despatch; that the money would be his and his wife's; that the world would be a very different and brighter sphere for him without any more trouble on his own account; that the shoes were outside the door, and the door closing on Samuel for good.

'I shouldn't mind,' said Mr. Crocketty, thoughtfully; 'a man has a right to enjoy the remainder of his life his own way. And you're pretty well off as it is, Filkin, and doing well; and there's nobody for me to consider.'

'I'm on the brink of pauperism, sir,' said Mr. Filkin, as his father-in-law handed him the trumpet for a reply.

'We've never been able to put anything by for advancing years, father,' added his daughter, with a quaver in her voice ; ' we relied upon you.'

'I should have thought, with all that coffin-making and burying, you had waxed fat, Filkin,' said his father-in-law, reproachfully ; 'and managed to put something by for a rainy day. But some people never will be provident. It isn't in them. I was always of a saving turn myself.'

' So it seems,' muttered Uncle Filkin.

' And I mean to begin saving again. I'm sure I shan't live up to my income, and, if I'm spared a few years, round will come the money again. Don't you see that, both of you ?'

'I can't see anything. My head's in a whirl.'

But presently—a few days afterwards, when Samuel Crocketty was about again—Mr. Filkin and his wife saw things with greater clearness. They accepted the position with a sigh, and looked the whole matter carefully and 'critically in the face. It became thoroughly impressed upon minds not too capacious or ductile that it was absolutely necessary to take great care of Mr. Crocketty—that no pains should be spared

M 2

to promote the health and comfort of an elderly gentleman with the handsome annual income of two thousand five hundred pounds, which expired with him.

The first day that Mr. Crocketty was 'like his usual self' was an event in his life—it was so strongly marked by the care and thoughtful kindness of his son-in-law. Mr. Crocketty was standing on the steps of the front door, pulling on a gouty pair of Berlin gloves, and preparing to set forth for that customary 'constitutional' in which he had regularly indulged before the last severe cold had interfered with his programme. It was a grey January day, with the clouds ominously thick overhead, and a cutting east wind tearing down the street at double-quick time, as if anxious to get out of it.

Mr. Filkin skipped to the door with unwonted alacrity.

'You're surely not thinking of going out—for the first time, too, after that bad cold—on such a day as this, sir?' he asked, in grave astonishment.

'I've been indoors long enough, Filkin,' replied his father-in-law. 'I am pining for fresh air.'

'The wind is in the east.'

' " An eager and a nipping air," Filkin,' quoted old Crocketty, 'but I fancy I shall enjoy it.'

' And—great heavens, sir, are you aware you are going out without an umbrella ?'

' I don't think it will rain.'

' It may rain at any moment. I'm sure it will rain. For mercy's sake don't go too far on such an uncertain day as this. Selina,' he bawled out, ' Mrs. Filkin—Bloggs—where *is* Mr. Crocketty's umbrella ?'

Selina brought it to him, and he took it with an odd, grim smile.

' Thank you,' he said ; ' perhaps I had better have it with me.'

' And, father, love,' remarked his daughter, hanging fondly on his left shoulder, ' you must take care of your poor, dear old throat, you know. That top button must not be unfastened —I'm sure it mustn't. There !'

And after being buttoned up to the throat,

and patted fondly between the shoulders, he
was allowed to depart, Mr. Filkin and his wife
watching him for awhile from the vantage-
ground of the top step.

'Where's he going now?' I heard Mr. Filkin
say.

'I think he said something about the city,' responded his better half.

'Why on earth can't he keep out of the city,'
growled the undertaker. 'He'll be run over
crossing the roads one of these fine days, and
then what the devil are we going to do?'

'You should go with him, Filkin.'

'He wouldn't have me.'

'Selina might go, when we could spare her.'

'Oh, no!' said Uncle Filkin, very shortly; 'not
Selina.'

It was on the cards that Samuel Crocketty
might think too much of Selina Filkin—save up
his money for her, if he lived long enough to
save anything—set her, in his estimation, before
his own flesh and blood. I was a trouble to my
uncle and aunt just then—a something in the
way—a snake in the grass almost—and they

were not kind to me, and said hard things of me
behind my back to Mr. Crocketty, until he told
them sharply that he did not believe one word
they said against me, and that he never would.
After which they were silent; but they loved
me none the more, and they seemed waiting
their opportunity to do me an ill turn. Hard to
confess this, but it was true, as it afterwards
appeared, and as I felt that I knew already. They
had been never kind to me; they had constituted
me for years their drudge; they had never made
this place home, or me happy within it; they
had been often absolutely unkind; but I had
struggled on with them and held my ground,
and done my best to be of service. But if it had
not been for Richard Richardson—but there, he
hardly belongs to this story, hero as he was to
me, good, faithful, honest husband as he afterwards became, thanks to Mr. Samuel Crocketty's
consideration for us in a little difficulty that came
later on.

Next month was Mr. Crocketty's birthday.
He had reached the honourable age of seventy-
one on the fourteenth of the month—Valentine's

day—and the day was kept with much rejoicing.

'I never felt so well in my life,' he remarked that evening; 'what do you say?' he added, handing my uncle the trumpet.

'I am glad to hear you say so,' replied his son-in-law; 'you are looking extremely well.'

'I really think I am,' he said, getting up, and clinging to the parlour mantelpiece to have a good look at himself, his daughter propping him up in the back for fear he should fall. 'I am cheating Time. The great leveller has forgotten me,' he added, magniloquently.

'Don't mention him. Keep him out of your thoughts. Keep yourself cheerful, Mr. Crocketty,' urged his son-in-law.

'I will.'

'Take another glass of port, sir. This is "Mahogany's Famous Nourishing Port."'

'Where did you get it?'

'At the "Compasses," over the way.'

'What did you give for it?' he asked, doubtfully.

'Three shillings and sixpence. A long price,' added the frugal Filkin.

'I bought a dozen or two of '47 port the other day. You'll find them upstairs. Two hundred and sixty shillings a dozen. Selina, fetch down a couple of bottles.'

'Two hundred and sixty shillings a dozen! Oh, gracious! I would be a little more careful with my money, sir, if I were you. Two hun——'

'If I cannot indulge in a luxury or two on an income of two thousand five hundred a-year,' spluttered forth Samuel Crocketty, indignantly, 'I should like to know who could!. Tell me that, Gregory Filkin, and don't talk to me as if I were a poor wretch of a custom-house officer with a beggarly pension. As if—as if——'

'My dear sir, don't excite yourself like this— over a trifle, too. You've a perfect right to do what you like with your own money. I haven't a word to say to the contrary.'

'It's a good job you haven't, Filkin,' said the old man, calming down.

He was quite himself when a bottle of '47 had been opened, and almost hilarious after he and Filkin had finished it. Perhaps he was a trifle too emotional, for his daughter regarded him anxiously, and, when little evidences of forethought were displayed in the shape of birthday gifts, he shed a few tears at their delicate suggestiveness. Mr. Filkin had bought him a stout pair of india-rubber goloshes, and his daughter had been absolutely lavish in her expenditure over an electrical chest-protector that had to be put on warm, and wound up, like an eight-day clock, once a week.

'And what have *you* got for me, Selina?' he inquired, quite sharply, as he almost pitched his trumpet at me; 'I did not think you would have utterly forgotten the old encumbrance.'

'Don't say "encumbrance," father,' said Mrs. Filkin.

'I have put a little pipe upon your dressing-table,' I said. 'I—I did not like to bring it down. It's a briar-wood pipe you admired in the tobacconist's next door a little while ago.'

'Good girl! Go and fetch it. I'll smoke it in honour of the donor.'

'Do you think smoking is good for you so late at night?' inquired his daughter.

'Good or bad, I'll smoke it.'

'It always makes you cough.'

'I don't care if I cough my heart up,' was the abrupt reply. 'Selina, get that pipe directly.'

When the pipe was in his hand, he looked at me very strangely from under his shaggy white brows, and said,

'I'm glad you haven't forgotten me. I was wondering if you would.'

'I thought she would,' remarked Mr. Filkin.

'I was sure she would,' added my aunt, 'for she never thinks of anybody or anything.'

'Except herself?' added Mr. Crocketty, interrogatively.

At which remark the Filkins laughed very much, as at a capital and well-timed *bon-mot.* They absolutely roared with laughter.

Later on, Mr. Crocketty said, when the subject appeared to have been forgotten,

'And I won't forget *your* birthday, Selina. When is it?'

'Oh! not till next September, sir.'

'That's a long time to wait, child. I may have been drawing on the stock before then,' he said, nodding his head towards the coffins in the shop.

'Don't go on like that, sir, for mercy's sake,' entreated Mr. Filkin, with a strong shudder. 'You must not get such nasty thoughts as that into your head. They're depressing; they're lowering in tone.'

He did not hear his son-in-law's protest.

'Next September,' he muttered; 'Selina's birthday. What's the date of it?'

'The twenty-ninth,' I replied, down the ear-trumpet.

'I shan't forget it. Not likely. My quarterly payment is due that day, you see.'

And he did not forget it though he was very ill when the time came round; though he was at death's door again, with all of us very anxious about him; though he had been well, and strong and cheerful all the spring and summer, and even to the beginning of this autumn, when the first cold wind caught him coming down the street again, and goloshes, and comforters, and electric chest-protectors were all of no avail to him.

The Filkins were prostrated with grief. When the decree was promulgated that Samuel Crocketty must keep to his bed, and would require the greatest care to pull through, a terrible anxiety seized upon the worthy couple.

'It's what I have been fearing all along,' groaned Filkin. 'I knew he wasn't a strong old man; that he was breaking fast; that his legs wouldn't keep him up much longer. He's off now; you see if he ain't. The doctor says as much.'

'He has been as bad as this before,' said the wife.

'Yes; but it's our luck, this is. A pretty fine thing those annuity vagabonds have made out of us.'

'I call it shameful,' said Mrs. Filkin.

'I call it a damned swindle,' said her lord and husband, biting at his finger-nails in his vexation.

On the twenty-ninth of September, my birthday, there was not much hope for Samuel Crocketty. He was looking very sadly. His faint, feeble, far-off words to me when I came into the room were—

'Many happy returns of the day, Selina Filkin.'

I took up the ear-trumpet, and responded.

'Thank you, Mr. Crocketty,' I replied. 'Oh, thank you.'

'What—what are you going to do with yourself to-day?' he asked, in little puffs of inquiry, finding his breath very hard to manage.

'I haven't thought of doing anything.'

'Aren't you going out with Richardson?'

'Oh, no; I can't be spared.'

'How's he getting on?

'I don't think he's getting on particularly well.'

'I wish he had a little more dash about him,' he reflected. 'Perhaps he will, when he's married. I should like you and him to get married before the year is out, Selina.'

'Why, we are hardly thinking about such nonsense.'

'Aren't you though?' he responded, in a surprised sort of manner. 'That's curious. How old are you to-day?'

'Twenty-two.'

'Quite time you were married,' he said. 'I hope you'll see about it.'

Aunt Filkin came in at this juncture, and looked from her father to me very sharply and inquisitively.

'What are you two talking about?' she said, in her old disagreeable manner. 'You know, father, you're to be kept quiet—very quiet.'

'I shall be quiet enough for anybody present-ly,' was the grim response.

'Filkin wants to know if you've had any letter this morning?' she inquired, through the usual medium of communication.

'What does he want to know that for?'

'You ought to have had a letter from the annuity-office, he says.'

'Ah! yes, with my quarter's allowance,' re-marked the old man; 'what a memory that Filkin has. But it's all right.'

'All right!'

'It has gone to my solicitors,' he replied, 'in

payment for a little bit of house-property for
Selina ; her birthday present.'

'What's that you say?' half shrieked his
daughter.

'I have bought Richardson's shop in Selina's
name. A dead bargain for six hundred pounds.
I have been about it for the last two months.
Richardson will get on very well '—he explained,
with difficulty, and taking much time over it
—'with Selina for his landlady.'

'Father, you are wandering!' exclaimed Mrs.
Filkin ; 'you would never rob your own family
in this way, you——'

'Selina is one of the family,' he said; 'the
best of the lot of you. I always promised her
something on her birthday. My income is too
large for me,' he continued, 'and I want to do
something with it.'

'Oh, Mr. Crocketty!' I exclaimed, 'who
would have thought of this. I don't deserve it
—I really don't deserve it.'

'You do not,' said my aunt, decisively; 'and
you'll never be mean enough to take it.'

'Ye-es,' I answered, hesitatingly, 'I think I'll

take it, for Richard's sake. And, dear Mr. Crocketty, I am so very much obliged to you.'

'Mr. Crocketty is not answerable for his actions just now,' said Aunt Filkin; 'it won't hold good in law.'

' What's that you say ?'

'It won't hold good in law !' she shouted at him.

'Yes, it will,' replied Mr. Crocketty; 'it's beautifully arranged. The deeds are quite ready at Parsons, 495, Bedford Row, drawn out in your name as the purchaser, Selina, and you'll have to go there at twelve o'clock this morning and just affix your signature. Parsons understands all about it. He's a very sensible fellow, is Parsons; he will take care of the deeds for you for awhile.'

' Oh ! if Filkin was home to fight my battles for me !' moaned my aunt.

' Where *is* Filkin ?' asked my benefactor, curiously.

' He's over at the " Compasses "—drowning his grief,' she sobbed forth ; 'he does not bear up at all.'

'Is he so sorry I'm ill?' asked Mr. Crocketty, in faint surprise. 'Poor fellow—is he though?'

'He's sorry you're not likely to recover; we have a good many bills to meet, and his Building Society is in a bad way, and is making calls on him—and he feels you've been the cause of his ruin, father.'

'Does he, indeed?'

'Yes; he does.'

'Well, he need not make a fuss about it till I am gone. It's very likely I shall get over this. I have had plenty of these attacks before, haven't I?' he inquired.

'You have, father. And each one's worse than the last. And they knew about that, the thieves, when they took all your money for the annuity,' whimpered his daughter.

'They haven't done badly,' he said, after a moment's consideration of this view of the case; 'it has been an excellent bargain for them. And I have not done badly either. I have lived all the longer for it.'

He looked hard at his daughter, but she was sobbing behind her handkerchief and making for the door. When she had withdrawn, he said, eagerly,

'Go straight to the lawyer's at once, Selina, and get that little job finished. And then marry that sleepy Richardson as soon as you can manage it, and rouse him, girl, rouse him. He's been too much alone there with his groceries. And you're not happy here, are you?'

'Not very happy.'

'There, be off then. And many happy returns of the day to you, Selina, and—thank you.'

'Thank me! for what, sir?'

'For taking care of old Sam Crocketty, and seeing his relations did not step too quickly into his shoes. Selina.'

'Yes, sir.'

'If I should get over this, do you think Dick Richardson would mind having me for a lodger?'

'I'm sure he would be very glad and proud, sir.'

'I'll take the first-floor front at a pound a week.'

'Oh! sir,' I cried, amazed at this business arrangement.

'Attendance included,' he added; 'and if I don't get over this—why, Filkin will bury me decently. There's enough money in that top drawer to pay his bill, and leave him a little for himself. More than he deserves.'

'You must not talk so, sir.'

'I am talking too much, I daresay. But there, there,' he added, settling himself comfortably in bed, 'go to old Parsons and sign the deeds, and step into your property; and kiss the old man before you go, young woman.'

I stooped over him and kissed him, and there was a strange, wistful look in his eyes that I had never seen before.

That I never saw again, poor Crocketty! For when I came back from Bedford Row, quite a landed proprietor, and independent at last of Uncle and Aunt Filkin, there were three of the shop shutters up, and all the blinds were down before the upstairs windows, and Uncle Filkin and his assistant Bloggs were hard at work in the back premises hammering and tapping vigorously, as though it were a match against time to get Samuel Crocketty as speedily as possible out of the way.

FRIENDS FROM THE CLOUDS.

FRIENDS FROM THE CLOUDS.

CAN a woman be considered so very, very old at three-and-thirty? Is it, after all, so great an age? Is it such a long, long distance from the days of youth and beauty? Are the hills so tremendously high between thirty-three and the maiden charms of sweet seventeen that the former is shut irremediably in Shadow-land? I do not believe it.. I may have been talked into this theory at one time—my worst time!—read into it by silly, sentimental novels, sung into it by sillier, sentimental ballads; but I know better now. At the present hour I am a little older in years and a great deal younger in thought and feeling than I was, and the reason for all this is the theme of my story.

To begin with, in my early days I had been crossed in love—not so deeply crossed that its marks had sunk into my face and scored it with as many lines as a railway map, but I had *had* my love troubles and my disappointments, and was not by any means the better for them. My lover had been no more of a hero than I had been a heroine—we were not of the stuff that the heroic comes from, although he had talked a great deal—an unnecessarily great deal—of *his* family, of *his* family connections, and of *his* great uncle, who was knighted for doing something intensely shabby to lug a gentleman into Parliament whose seat was slipping unpleasantly from under him during a great political contest for an especially rotten ' division.' But Arthur always talked like a hero, even when he was young and wore turn-down collars, and my girl's heart took his speech for silvern and went out to meet his rather more than half-way. What a waste of time and years and pretty compliments it was, after all! My brother, my senior by twelve years, stepped between us, took a dislike to Arthur, snapped him up, and told him plainly that he was a ' conceited, stuck-up, overgrown, knock-kneed puppy '—Arthur was six feet one, and *did* give way a little at the knees—and made things so disagreeable all round that Arthur told me one summer evening that he thought it was better that we should part.

Probably it *was* better. It was vexatious, however, to think some time afterwards that my brother was in the right, and that I might have had a bad time with Arthur had I married him, and that I was mercifully spared the fate of Arthur's actual wife—he married a brewer's widow, who sued for a judicial separation some three years after that, and got it easily—and that I might have done worse than become my brother's housekeeper and general factotum in his desolate little house at Rumney Burn, in Lancashire.

My brother William was perfectly right, but he need not have impressed that fact upon me quite so often, and at such uncalled-for times; and he might have impressed me with more suavity of demeanour and kindly consideration for my woman's feelings. But then he had no suavity of demeanour, and—I blush to confess this of my only relation—his kindly consideration was chiefly for himself. He was not altogether a hard brother, but he had immense faith in his own convictions and an immense contempt for everybody else's. He was always right, and other folk were always wrong. The reader may have met a character like this in his pilgrimage through life. I have heard of one being seen as far west of England as Land's End, and there is a curious specimen, I have been informed on the best authority, at the Old Fogies' Club, Pall Mall. This makes three altogether to my certain knowledge. But brother William had been successful in life, and thought he had a right to crow, although he did not make any friends by his crowing. No one cared particularly for William Ironstone. In our own part of the world he was put down as cantankerous. No one seemed at all anxious for his society, though society of any kind was scarce enough at Rumney Burn; and he certainly displayed no

anxiety for society himself. He was almost a
Timon of Athens in a drab suit and gaiters, and
with a hat three sizes too large for him.

William was content with himself and his
surroundings—at least, he said so—and that was
sufficient for all times and seasons. He had his
own way, and waxed fat and thrived, and save
a little doggedness when the wind was easterly,
and an extra degree of crabbedness when his
liver was askew, he was not altogether an un-
reasonable being. Why he did not like society
—he had snubbed the vicar of the church, and
insulted the solicitor and doctor of the next
town within three months of our settling down
at Rumney Burn—I was never quite able to
fathom. Certainly it struck me that he had had
his disappointment at sometime or other when
I was a little girl, and had taken to business
habits to get over it, as weaker-minded men
would have taken to poetry or brandy.

And business habits had made him staid and
old-fashioned, and rich and methodical—and
friendless, utterly. His method was astonishing
—everything was regulated by square and rule

at the Cedars, Rumney Burn. Woe to the
servants who were five minutes behind time
with the breakfast in the morning, or went to
bed five minutes later than usual in the evening.
Woe to the cook who did not dish up the dinner
to the exact hour appointed, to the coachman
who was not ready with the carriage to the
precise second which had been mentioned for an
airing, to the gardener who did not set his
plants and shrubs, and prune his trees, according
to the time for planting and pruning as regulated by William Ironstone, whose manner in life
was to regulate everything within his own
domain. Was it to be wondered at that I should
fall in with his regulations and get methodical a
little bit myself, and feel weighed down by
those three-and-thirty years I have already mentioned, despite my inner consciousness which
should have assured me that, under more
favourable surroundings, there were life, and
enjoyment of life, and an autumn of youth left
to me before pert folk could say that I was
getting ' so dreadfully old " ?

Of course, I began to look old—a pale reflection of my brother without his drab suit and gaiters—and to think in my heart of hearts that it was a neutral-tinted world in which I was playing my small part out. Brother William had no such ideas of self-disparagement, and that I should imagine for one instant that his company was not sufficient solace for my declining years had never entered into the wildest dream of his imagination.

I wonder what William Ironstone would have done without his big garden, and his cedars, of which he was inordinately vain, as though he had planted them and seen them grow up to their big, broad-spreading, funereal proportions, instead of buying them ready made along with the rest of the fixings? He was fonder of his garden than of me; it was his solace and distraction, his one study. He did more work than his three gardeners put together; he was always out of doors.

'There's old Bill Ironstone upside down again,' I heard an irreverent postman say to the coachman one morning, as he caught sight of my brother weeding his garden path; and certainly,

in the garden, it was difficult to discover my
brother in anything like a dignified posture.
Dahlias were his chief delight. He spent a great
deal of money upon dahlias, and people could
flatter him on that point when they could not
draw a smile or a sympathetic glance from him
on any other topic under the sun. In the evening,
in the autumn time, when the weather was not
always of the warmest, he would sit before his
grandest bed of dahlias, smoke his pipe, and pose
as the monarch of all he surveyed. He was at
his best then ; he had dined well, he had got over
the little vexations of the day, and it was his
pleasure to take his ease in his garden ground
and admire his flowers, and endeavour to listen
to my housekeeping experiences of the last six
hours. He was not a sociable man, but he
strongly objected to sitting in his garden alone.
He preferred me near him, knitting or netting,
'in the gloaming.' There were times when I
used to fancy he was getting nervous as he was
getting old, but that was all fancy, I daresay.

One evening, early in September, we were in
the summer-house after dinner—always an hour

after dinner by the chronometer he carried, and which never varied a minute in a month—and I remember it was extra cold and bleak, even for September in Lancashire. It was growing dusk.

'What are you shivering at, Priscilla?' he asked, suddenly; 'you know I strongly object to see anybody shiver.'

'It's rather cold this evening.'

'I don't feel it a bit. You must have something the matter with you, if you call this cold.'

'I mean it is rather cold for the time of year. I have known September such a warm month,' I added, with my teeth chattering.

'I don't remember a warmer September than this has been, or a finer evening than this. There really is not anything to shiver at, Priscilla,' he said, reproachfully. 'I wish to goodness you would leave off rattling.'

'Perhaps if I walked about a bit——'

'Ah! go and walk. Do something,' he said.

I walked the whole extent of the garden grounds, and then returned to the summer-house.

My brother was half dozing, and gave quite a little start when I came back to his side.

'I have disturbed your nap, William.'

'I haven't been asleep,' he answered, shortly. ' I never sleep in the open air—you know I don't. Do you think I want to wake up stone blind?'

'I beg your pardon. I thought you were nodding, William.'

' You were mistaken, Priscilla,' he said. ' You are always mistaken, for the matter of that.'

'Perhaps I am.'

'There is no perhaps about it—you are.'

' Very well,' I said, a little tetchily, 'I am, so there's an end of it.'

He was extra cross and snappish that evening, and so was I. He had had nothing to disturb his equanimity that day, save two circulars from Manchester asking for subscriptions for local charities and seventeen prospectuses soliciting his immediate application for shares in seventeen separate swindles of colossal proportions. Possibly something in the air had disturbed us —at all events something in the air was to disturb us both, and that very shortly. But we

recked not of the great change approaching; indeed, as if to mark the contrast, my brother said
suddenly, and with a flourish of his long clay
pipe,

'What I admire about this place, Priscilla, is
its perfect state of repose.'

'It's a little dull, William; especially at this
time of year.'

'I see nothing dull in it,' he answered; 'I
don't think any well-balanced mind would see
anything dull in it at any time, more especially
at this time. What *do* you want?'

'I hardly know,' I answered, with a sigh.

'Here's everything the heart can wish for,' he
continued; 'no noise and bustle, and smoke and
smother, and fuss and excitement.'

'No; nothing at all of that kind. That's very
true.'

'Thirty miles away from a big town—perfect
peace, and rest, and seclusion—not harassed by
a crowd of busybodies of neighbours, people
who drop down upon you at all hours and seasons,
and always at the time and season when you
would give anything rather than see their ugly

faces. Absolute rest there is, Priscilla, and yet you are not content.'

'I am not of a dissatisfied nature, William, but——'

'Perfect rest and—what the devil is that?'

And what the devil was it, I could have said myself the instant afterwards, and without considering that I was actually profane.

We both sprang to our feet, looked wildly round, edged a little closer to each other for mutual protection, stared into each other's face, and gasped for breath in our complete bewilderment. Suddenly there were branches of trees and hedges ominously cracking. There was a strange rushing and hissing noise. There was a stranger flopping and flapping, as of gigantic wings, a distant crackling of wood, and the voices of men in high altercation, and making use of bad words—indubitably bad words.

My first impression was that our gardeners had been seized with temporary derangement, and were fighting amongst themselves, and with all available missiles within reach; but that delusion was dispelled by their sudden rush into

the open air and from the outhouse where they
had been packing up their implements.

'Oh, lor a mussy, sir—what's the matter?'

Then the voices in the distance went on
again.

'Look out—catch hold—hold hard—let go
that confounded rope—oh! blazes. Now then!
No—not now. Oh!—whoop. Let go now!
No—hold hard, you confounded jackass, you!
Hold hard, I tell ye!'

And then, with an immense bound and more
bobbing and flopping and flapping, a monster
balloon, dishevelled and short of breath, or gas,
and knocked out of all shape by contact with
rough earth—a most disreputable looking, out-
all-night, all-of-one-side balloon—came skidding
and bobbing and rolling and swaying like a
drunken giant into the garden, and scurried at
a rapid rate across the grass-plot and the flower
beds. A malformed, untidy, and drunken balloon
it surely was.

'Here, lend a hand some of ye fellows, and
don't stand gaping there. Catch hold of the
ropes, will ye?' called some one from the car.

'Mind the grappling irons—whew! We're off again, by gord!'

And away the balloon shot past us, the inmates of the car bawling incomprehensible instructions to Mr. Ironstone—who had become purple with rage, and was shaking his stick at them—and then out came all the dahlias by their roots, which became entangled in the claws of the grappling irons trailing below the car, and were borne off with their garish heads upside down in one clean swoop.

'Well, of all the——'

But there was no time to listen to my brother's comments on the exciting events which were passing beneath our notice. The balloon was still skidding along some eight feet from the ground, till it was brought up against the greenhouse roof, the glass of which the grappling irons smashed neatly and expeditiously; then away it went with a bound like an india-rubber ball to earth again, and shaved from a side bed about thirty feet of scarlet geraniums, and finally came driving towards the summer-house, into which my brother and I, and the three gardeners,

all tore for our lives. It struck the summer-
house, was again whirled backwards, and got
jammed amongst the branches of the cedars,
where it looked like a live thing struggling to
have another 'shy' at us. The gardeners crept
timidly to the rescue after sundry objurgations
hurled at them by the senior person in the car,
and presently the balloon was hauled with difficulty to earth, everybody tumbling over everybody else, and the gas escaping with most unpleasant distinctness.

'Ye'll be after putting that pipe out, sorr, or
we shall be blown to atoms before we know
where we are,' cried the aeronaut to my brother,
when he and his companion were out of the car,
shaking themselves, and facing us on *terra
jirma*.

'Lord help us—what do you mean by all
this, sir?' shouted my brother, pitching his
long clay several yards from him immediately.
'Whatever has brought you into this neighbourhood with that dangerous lump of tom-
foolery?'

The aeronaut was an Irishman, and had a

sense of humour in him as well as a sense of dignity.

'The south-west breeze brought us here. I'm Captain Gray, sorr, of whom ye've doubtless heard.'

'No; I have not, sir.'

'Then ye're living a strangely isolated life, sorr, and I pity ye; and I'll talk to ye when I have got my balloon more ship-shape. On my conscience, Bigweed, but we have done the balloon a mighty deal of damage this time, and no mistake.'

'It doesn't matter in the least,' said his companion, in so bass a voice that even my brother was startled, and gave a quick glance in the last speaker's direction. Mr. Bigweed was a young man by comparison with the weather-beaten, grey-whiskered aeronaut at his side; a very tall, thin, round-shouldered young man who wore coloured spectacles, the left glass of which had been shaken out of its frame, and gave him an odd, one-eyed aspect.

'But it does matter, Mr. Bigweed, as the damage is my affair, and I went up taking all risks,' said the aeronaut. 'It matters a great deal.'

'It shall not cost you a penny,' remarked the young man, in a deeper voice still; 'you will please to consider this my affair. I persuaded you to start. It was all my fault.'

'All right; if ye look at it in that light, I'm obliged to you,' said the aeronaut, lightly.

'And—and who's responsible for the damage done to *my* property,' spluttered forth my brother, indignantly; 'just look at the wreck you have made all over the place with your cussed balloon. That was a dahlia bed once, sir, and there were ten yards of scarlet geraniums over there, and the greenhouse glass, and the cedars —good God! it's like an earthquake!'

'I must confess we've put things a little bit out of sorts here, sorr,' said the Irishman, 'and ye'll allow me to apologise. I had not the least intention of intruding. If I could have dropped on the hillside it would have been preferable, but the wind carried us over your wall, and so, being at the mercy of the wind, here we are, sorr. And you will allow me to say,' he added, with considerable dignity, 'that, as a rule, we are generally made welcome by the gentlemen in the vicinity of our sphere of location, and not bullied and treated as pick-pockets, sorr! I may say that by the *gentlemen* in the vicinity into which it is our fortune to drop we are treated as gentlemen—as we hope we are, sorr. And now, perhaps, ye'll not keep on jabbering and distracting my attention whilst I have this machine to get into something like order, and if your men will find us some lanterns—for it's getting moighty dark—why, the sooner we shall be able to rid ye of our ugly presence, don't ye see?'

My brother thrust his hands to the depths of his pockets, and looked down at his gaiters, and seemed to be taken a little aback by the outpourings of this indignant and satirical aeronaut.

'The gardeners will do all that you require,' he muttered.

'Many thanks, sorr,' said the aeronaut, taking off a hat very much knocked out of shape; 'and if ye'll instruct one of your men to run for a

conveyance—a big van or a strong cart is best
—I shall be still further obliged to ye.'

'Run for a conveyance! Where the deuce
do you think a man is going to run to about
here?'

'Isn't there a village——'

'Seven miles off there's a village,' I ventured
to remark; 'but I doubt if there's any conveyance to be got.'

'Is there not a farm, madam, or something
about?'

'Not within seven miles. It is principally
moorland in this neighbourhood.'

'What a God-forsaken part of the world!'
muttered the aeronaut. 'Why, this would suit
ye, Bigweed, to a T. Well, we must pack up
the balloon and send for it to-morrow, and walk
that seven miles—we must, old man. There's
no help for it.'

'I can't walk seven yards,' said his bass-
voiced friend.

'Eh! what's the matter wi' ye?'

'I've put something out—instep-bone, or
something. It doesn't matter. Go on with the

work,' said the phlegmatic young man ; 'don't mind me.'

'But how are you going to get on ?'

'I'm not trying to get on. And,' he added, the instant afterwards, 'I can't get on. And it doesn't matter, really.'

He limped his way into the summer-house, where he sat down very composedly. The aeronaut looked after him, scratched his head in a puzzled manner, and then busied himself with the balloon and the gardeners, and was altogether so extremely energetic that he quite forgot my brother and myself standing and watching the operations.

'I don't quite see what they'll do,' I whispered to my brother.

'I don't care what they do, so that I get them off my premises,' muttered William Ironstone.

'But how are they to get away? And how is the lame gentleman——'

'He has no business to be lame, has he, on my property? If he's idiot enough to trust himself in a balloon with that mad Irishman, that's his look-out.'

'But if he can't walk we must have the carriage out, and——'

'What! *My* carriage for this couple of mountebanks and their blackguard balloon! Never.'

'But——'

'Priscilla, hold your tongue,' snapped up my brother. 'I'm going into the house. I'll have nothing more to do with this absurd business. I leave it to you to see them off the premises as speedily as possible.'

'Any refreshment?'

'Refreshment be ——; no, no refreshment. A likely thing, after all the damage that they've done. What next, I wonder?'

He was not left to wonder long. He was walking away towards the house, crosser than ever now that he had had time to reflect upon the enormity of the whole surprising proceedings, when Captain Gray, who had found time to put a few questions to the gardeners, skipped across the lawn, planted himself in front of my brother, and stopped his progress—indeed, nearly brought him to his knees on the gravel—by two emphatic slaps with two big hard hands on my brother's two shoulders.

'What, Bill! Bill Ironstone—after all these years, old Billy?'

'Bless my soul, sir! what next will you do? How dare you, sir? What——'

'I'm Teddy—Teddy Gray—were not we boys together at old Spanker's school at Liverpool? —young men, old pals—didn't I go to sea, and leave ye head over heels in love with my sister, and didn't ye have a row after I had left ye both, and break off the match, and all before I could get back to make the peace between ye? Old Billy Ironstone, there's no forgetting that. I'm right glad to see you again, Bill—upon my soul I am! Shake hands once again, Billy. Why, this is just like a mealy-drama altogether.'

And Captain Gray seized hold of my brother's two hands—one with a stick in it—and pumped his arms up and down, and fairly bewildered him with so much exuberance, and such genuine pleasure and surprise at seeing him.

'Are you—are you Edward Gray, then?' my brother gasped forth at last.

' To be sure I am.'

' Of Liverpool ?'

' Sure, and haven't I just said so ?'

' I shouldn't have known you.'

' Nor I you,' said the aeronaut. ' You've got beastly fat, Bill.'

' You're not particularly thin, that I can see,' replied my brother, quickly.

' Ay, no ; we've both made flesh since we walked about Lime Street without a penny to fly with, either of us. Bill, ye were a good-looking young sprig then, and that's more than I can say now, and be truthful. And ye had a much better temper of your own then, Bill, and were a good sort of a fellow, and—but I *am* glad to catch hold of your fist once more for all that. 'Pon my conscience, but I am !'

My brother's face twitched spasmodically. This friend from the clouds—from the far-off days when he was young, good-looking, and poor, when I was a little girl—was too much for his imperturbability, his natural hardness, his dislike of men and women in the aggregate. He was for once not his customary self. It was many years back in his life since anyone had been glad to see him. It was a novelty that impressed him by its very strangeness, and the flattery which it conveyed was genuine, and took him off his guard.

'It's very surprising. Bless my soul and body! Ted Gray,' he muttered, 'I thought that you were dead and buried long ago.'

'They told me you were dead when I asked about you in Liverpool.'

'The liars!'

He turned back with Captain Gray, and, as if ashamed of any exhibition out of his usual run of stoicism, said, a little more roughly,

'Get on with your balloon, and then—and then,' he added, after an anxious pause, 'we'll have a bit of supper before you and your friend start. Priscilla,' turning to me, 'will you see about supper for these gentlemen?'

'Certainly, with pleasure;' and I hurried away before he should alter his mind. I thought that he had come into the house to alter it when I found him standing at my side in the dining-room a quarter-of-an-hour afterwards.

'There—there isn't time for a hot supper, I suppose, Priscilla?' he asked, with almost a blush on his face at his own suggestion.

'Oh, dear, no. And I am almost afraid there is not enough cold meat in the house, William.'

'Make it up with pickles; Ted was always a pig at pickles,' he remarked, as he stepped into the garden again.

Five minutes afterwards and he reappeared.

'How long shall you be now?'

'The servants will not be very long, William.'

'They're both in a hurry to get away. Especially the lame one, who I don't think is quite right in his head, mind. He talks such awful rot.'

'Does he though?' I said; 'but hadn't they better stay the night, and——?'

'Certainly not,' cried my brother, with alacrity; 'what next will you think of, to turn the place topsy-turvy? Let me know when supper is ready. I shall be precious glad when they're gone. You will find us in the garden. Gray's drinking whisky and water like a fish—I

VOL. III.   P never saw a man pour it down so. And Big-weed won't drink at all. He's infernally un-sociable.'

I looked attentively at William. It struck me that he was rather flushed, and that he flaunted his clay pipe about with a trifle too much ex-travagance of gesture. He had been drinking whisky and water too, and, although in strict moderation, he was not used to whisky. Not that he was the worse for liquor. On the con-trary, and presupposing that he was in liquor, I am ashamed to confess he was much the better for it. I had never seen him like this in all my life before.

When I went at last in search of the gentle-men, there was a fresh surprise for me. They were all seated under the cedars, before a little table on which were grog, and glasses, and cigars, and pipes, and Captain Gray was singing one of Moore's melodies in a burring, squeaking tone, like a man humming through a comb, and the bowls of the three pipes in the distance were aglow with fire. Quite a convivial garden-party.

'Then wreathe the bowl
With flowers of soul,
The brightest wit can find us ;
We'll take a flight
Tow'rds heaven to-night,
And leave dull earth behind us,'

sang the captain.

' "And leave dull earth behind us," ' quoted Mr. Bigweed, dismally. 'Too shoppy, Gray, too balloony altogether. Not my style of song at all.'

' Ye'd prefer a love-song, mayhap ?' said the other, with a most pronounced curl of his lip.

'I don't believe in love. You know I don't. Why revive——'

' Bill, m' boy,' cried the captain, turning to my brother, and without waiting for the conclusion of his friend's question, ' ye remember the song, and how vexed Lizzie was with you and me for singing it one night? And after all we got her to join in the chorus at last, and a rare fine evening we had of it altogether.'

'I remember,' said my brother, in a husky voice.

' Ay, bedad, we were happy enough then—

happy as kings, or as young puppies with their troubles to come, eh, Bill ?'

'Yes, perhaps so.'

'It was a Friday night—bad luck to Fridays! —and I had brought Donaldson home for the first time to supper.'

'You had.'

'That baste Donaldson, who turned out such a brute, Ted, and broke my sister's heart. Who would have believed that now, with the silky manners he had?' remarked the captain.

'I never liked him.'

'But she did, the silly creature. And as ye wouldn't open your mouth, and he was always opening his, why——'

'Ted, you're not getting on with your whisky,' said my brother, hastily. 'And here's Priscilla to tell us that supper is ready. Mr. Bigweed, how will you manage to get into the house ?'

'Don't mind me in the least,' was the reply. 'If you'll send me out a crust of dry bread and a drop of cold spring water, I shall do very well here, and I daresay shall be strong enough in the morning to leave your hospitable mansion on my hands and knees. Pray don't take any notice of me. I'm not worth it.'

'Bigweed, you're a melancholy idiot,' shouted forth the aeronaut. 'Catch hold of my old pal's arm, and limp yerself into the house somehow. And I'll lead the way with the lady, if she will allow me the inexpressible honour.'

He raised his hat, offered me his arm, and then hurried me towards the house at a brisk trot, as though he fancied the supper was hot, and might get cold before we reached the dining-room. But there was a method in his alacrity.

'Your brother Bill will take some time to get Bigweed along, Miss Ironstone,' he said; 'and I wanted to just say a word to ye in the strictest confidence, and if ye'll allow an old friend, as it were, of the family?'

I inclined my head, although I was half afraid of what he was going to say.

'I hope ye won't mind my friend Bigweed's manner,' he said, in a husky whisper; 'and that ye'll do your best to put up with him for half-an-hour or so. He's in a bad way.'

'Poor fellow. Is his instep——'

'No, his heart—not his instep, madam. He'll soon get over his instep, poor shrimp,' he replied, 'but he's met with a disappointment—badly jilted; and all the better for him, if he only knew. But his medical attendant says he must have distraction—excitement—to keep him up. He has taken to balloons to keep him up, but they don't have any effect. Only when they come down—then he's excited for five minutes or so—not longer. It's a bad complaint, though he's not a bad fellow.'

'It seems to me very distressing.'

'It is. If we could only rouse him—but I can't, and his family can't, and he gets softer every day. I am afraid of his doing something desperate.'

'Oh, good gracious!'

'And then he'll do it in such a dull, dead, ditch-water fashion that will take all the spirit out of it. If he blows his brains out, he'll do it flabbily—ye see if he doesn't.'

'I hope I shall never see anything of the kind,' I said, very firmly.

'Of course, of course, Miss Ironstone. That is a mere figure of speech of mine, to give ye an idea, as it were, of his character.'

'Yes, I think I understand,' I said. 'Was he so very deeply attached to the lady?'

'When I say his soul was bound up with her, it's a mere parcel-post kind of expression by comparison with his absorbing passion, ma'am,' replied Captain Gray; 'and she was undeserving of it all.'

'Dear, dear. How sad!'

'And he did not meet his disappointment like a man—like your brother, for instance.'

'N—no?' I said, interrogatively.

'Bill was brave throughout; he became hard, disagreeably hard probably, but hard.'

'He is a leetle disagreeable at times.'

'Not a doubt of that,' he added, confidentially, 'But, at all events, he bore up. And Bigweed doesn't bear up, not even in a balloon.'

'I'm sorry to hear it.'

'And, to tell you the truth, I'm getting tired of the custody of Mr. Bigweed; he palls upon one in a car five feet by three. But he *will*

come with me. And now he has met with an
accident. That will distract him, I hope, and
give him something fresh to think about. But
you will try to cheer him, Miss Ironstone, if
you can. Female society would do wonders for
such an impressionable man, if he would only
take to it again, the doctor says. Talk to him
at supper, and don't say or sing anything that is
sentimental, please, or he'll burst into tears and
spoil the blessed evening.'

Captain Gray was evidently looking forward
to a festive night of it. Fancy anything festive
at Rumney Burn !

'I'm afraid I shall not be able to keep particularly cheerful,' I said, timidly, 'I'm not naturally cheerful.'

'So I should think, ma'am. But I shall be
there to help you. *I'm* naturally cheerful.'

'So I should think,' I added, a little satirically
perhaps.

'That's why Bigweed's relations put that in-
cubus upon me,' he said. 'I was just the man,
full of life, and energy, and spirits, and go, they
said. And, by Jove, all my life, and energy,

and spirits are on the go with that fellow.
That's the melancholy result, Miss Ironstone, and
it's affecting me.'

Captain Gray was a trifle selfish after all. I
could only feel sympathy with the crippled
sufferer, lagging so far in the rear, and hanging
on to my brother, ' with all his infernal weight,'
as William said savagely afterwards.

We were sitting down to supper presently,
William and I facing each other at opposite
ends of the table, Mr. Bigweed on my right, and
Captain Gray on my brother's right, a very odd
party of four. In the lamplight, and without
his glasses, Mr. Bigweed improved; he was
very pale with long hair which had not been
cut for many, many months of his disconsolate
career. I was sure he wrote poems, and could
play upon some musical instrument, and his
brow was exceedingly classical, if marred a little
by bumps—temporary bumps, owing to the
balloon accident.

He afforded a strange contrast to his friend,
Captain Gray, who was as red as a pillar-box.

1 think I did exert myself that evening to be

cheerful after catching Captain Gray's expressive
eye once or twice, and my brother's wondering
eye, and the sad, tear-moistened, dark eye of
Percy Bigweed. I was always catching somebody's eye that evening, till, in my embarrass-
ment, it became a party that was all eyes.

And the eyes of Percy Bigweed became at
last the most embarrassing of the three pairs
before me—there was so yearning an interest in
them, as I learned long afterwards. I mean the
next day, before luncheon, when—but I am
precipitate.

The æronaut and my brother did the chief
part of the conversation, in a loud voice to
begin with, and to which no one paid the least
attention, till they dropped into half whispers
and mutterings, when Percy and I—how strange
to say 'Percy and I!'—tried hard to hear every
word they were saying. We did hear a little.
Captain Gray was telling my brother the whole
history of his unfortunate sister's marriage
career, and how badly she had been treated by
that brute of a Donaldson, before his premature
but fortunate decease at a steeplechase.

'And what's she doing now, Gray?' inquired my brother, with careless indifference, as it were.

'She keeps house and home for me, her bachelor brother, at Southport, whenever I am in Southport.'

'Beastly sandy place, Southport.'

'It is gritty.'

'And very lonely for her, with you away so much.'

'Yes, she pines a bit. But man, or woman, is made to pine.'

'That's true,' said Mr. Bigweed, with a deep sigh that stirred the flowers in the centre dish, and blew a spray of maidenhair fern into the salt-cellar; 'but why mention such a thing, at such a supper?'

'What's the matter with the supper?' said my brother, becoming suddenly acrimonious. A little would always put him out.

'It's the best we could do at a moment's notice, Mr. Bigweed,' I said, apologetically.

'It's a splendid supper,' he said, 'and I meant to imply it was a supper that I was very much enjoying. In the spirit,' he added, as we all looked at his plate full of the meat and pickles with which he had only trifled, ' in the spirit, and with such pleasant company round me.'

'Nately put, Bigweed, by the sowl of me,' cried the aeronaut.

' I don't eat suppers now, and 1 don't go into society now,' Mr. Bigweed still further explained, ' and the whole thing is a bit bewildering to one who is living for himself, in silence, and in solitude, and in—in Liverpool. I hardly seem to realise it yet,' and here he pressed his hand over his classical brow, and seemed counting every bump he had got there, and swept back his tangled mass of raven hair, and once more I caught his eye—both of his eyes, with a wonderful and dreamy glare in them which made me nervous. I looked away, when he brought my heart into my mouth, and caused my brother to stick his fork into his lip, by shouting forth in a loud voice, suddenly,

' Great heavens !'

' What the holy Moses is the matter now ?' cried the captain.

'I never saw such a likeness in my life to Matilda,' he exclaimed, excitedly. 'The very image, as she sits sideways.'

'Who sits sideways?' asked William.

'Your sister, Miss Ironbone.'

'Ironstone, sir, not bone.'

'I beg pardon, stone. Captain Grey, you see the likeness? You do see the likeness!'

'I thank my blessed stars that I never saw your Matilda in my life, sorr.'

'Ah! I had forgotten. Yes, it is a wonderful likeness; but it would have been better that I had died in the balloon than have revived such a terrible reminiscence as this. I shall go distracted,' he murmured; 'don't mind my emotion, please; take no notice of me—I will be calm presently—these gherkins are very good, ha! ha! you pickled them yourself, Miss Ironstone? Matilda—my Matilda no longer, but Jones's Matilda—was a great hand at home-made pickles. She did not believe in the things you buy in bottles. Not she.'

'Does he always go on like this?' I heard my brother ask his old friend the captain.

'Never knew him before. Just what I ima-
gined might happen. Just what will please his
family tremendously. He is shaking off his
inertia at last.'

'Hadn't he better go and shake it off in the
garden?' muttered William, back to him, 'I
don't like it here.'

'He'll be better after supper.'

'Priscilla,' said my brother at once, 'shall you
be much longer?'

I had not hurried. I was endeavouring to
keep Mr. Bigweed in countenance, who was not
hurrying either; in fact, who had hardly begun
his supper, and was waxing eloquent.

'It seems a remarkably strange thing, now
that I come to reflect upon it seriously,' he said,
'that here are four people, massed together, as
it were, who are all singularly lonely and miserable objects. Yes, we are all objects.'

'Spake for yourself, Mr. Bigweed,' said the
captain.

'I'm not miserable—who are you calling a
miserable object?' remarked my brother
William.

' I'm not lonely,' I ventured to add, as my own especial answer.

He set these protests all aside, waved them away, with both his arms in the air, as paltry excuses which he would have none of.

'You are miserable in your separate ways, though you hardly know it. I am miserable, and I do know it. That is the only difference between us. And you, sir,' turning suddenly to my brother, who jumped in his chair, and then edged himself more closely to the side of the captain, 'have known what it is to be severed —rudely severed, as it were—from the object of your affections——'

' When I was a young fool, sir. And I don't want that subject to be discussed just now, or at any time.'

' We are kindred souls, Mr. Ironstone ; we are both victims to the perfidy of woman,' said Mr. Bigweed.

' Where's the perfidy ?' cried the aeronaut. ' Bill Ironstone never proposed to my sister—she never knew that my friend here cared as much as a snap for her ; if she had, it might have

been a very different life for both of them, poor
things.'

'Gray, I object to being classed as a poor
thing,' said my brother, 'and I wish you would
not go on—in—in such an abominably foolish
way.'

'It is I, sir, who am to blame,' said Mr. Bigweed, politely, again. 'It was Matilda who
trifled with me, who spurned my suit, who—oh!
heaven and earth! how like you are to her now,
Miss Priscilla, with that sweet, pensive expression, and yet with an expression that is all your
own. Don't move. Pray don't move ?'

'Gray,' said my brother, with a groan, 'how
long will it be before you go home ?'

'Home, Bill! ye are jesting with me. Didn't
ye say in the garden that ye could put us both
up for the night, ye thought?'

'Yes, but I only thought ; and I'm quite sure
now that you had both better go away, and call
for the balloon in the morning.'

'My friend is helpless,' said the captain,
sternly, 'ye forget.'

'Yes, I am quite helpless, thank you,' added

Mr. Bigweed, complacently; 'don't cast me into the dark night. This is the first gleam of sunshine that for a long while I have seen fall across my chequered path.'

'Sunshine! in the dark night,' added the captain, with a wink at me which I resented with a frown. 'Bill, my boy, there is no help for it. We're fixtures, and the grog and the cigars are still out in the garden. And it's a beautiful evening, and not at all late.'

'But——'

'And while we are talking over old times, Miss Priscilla can sing or play, perhaps, to my invalid friend. That piano tells a pretty story, Miss Ironstone—eh, now?'

'Miss Ironstone, you sing!' shouted Mr, Bigweed, with enthusiasm—shouted so loudly that my brother regarded him again with dismay before retiring precipitately into the garden, followed by Captain Gray. But I was not afraid of him. I was interested in him. It had been dark night with him, he had said, until he had seen me. I was his gleam, my panting heart whispered to me softly.

How long I played and sang to Mr. Percy Bigweed I shall never know.

The rest is like a dream to me—a happy and strange dream. And Mr. Bigweed, who had dragged himself to the couch by the side of the piano, lay and watched my countenance, and listened with his eyes fixed on me, and his hands clasped together, and said softly, 'Another, if you will only sing another,' until I had got through—upon a moderate computation—some three and twenty ballads; and then my brother and the captain, both looking stolid and sleepy, returned into the house.

'Hush!' cried Mr. Bigweed reprovingly, as my brother stumbled over a footstool, 'Miss Ironstone is going to oblige us with a little song.'

'I think there has been enough squalling for a twelve-month,' said my brother.

'Oh! profanity,' cried Mr. Bigweed, 'she has a sweet voice. Matilda had a voice, but it was not so sweet as this. Hers was a little raspy. One more, Miss Ironstone.'

'It'll have to be to-morrow, then,' said my

brother. 'Good gracious, I haven't been up so late as this for twenty years.'

And so that happy and memorable evening came to an end. And the next morning Mr. Bigweed rang the bell and desired his compliments to Mr. Ironstone, and would he kindly send up the three gardeners to help to carry him downstairs to breakfast, as he was wholly unable to move without assistance.

'Here's a pretty go,' ejaculated Mr. Ironstone; 'what's to be done now?'

'Sam had better ride over to Dr. Smithies; Mr. Bigweed might have put something out.'

'He's put me out,' said my brother, 'I know that.'

Mr. Bigweed was carried downstairs like a Guy Fawkes, and set up to the breakfast-table. There they told him that a doctor was to be sent for.

He smiled at this.

'Thank you very much,' he said, 'I shall want looking to, I'm sure.'

Later on he said to me, with another strange smile illuming his expressive countenance,

'My foot is as big as a bushel-basket. I can't move. I'm so very glad.'

And then the poor dear sufferer fainted away.

Shall I go on? Is there any more to say at which the reader cannot guess? Hardly. A few lines, and the romance of Priscilla Ironstone is at an end. Mr. Percy Bigweed had put something out, and twisted something round, in his instep, and his was a serious case, involving much nursing and patient care, or the doctor would not answer for the consequences. And I was his nurse, and *I* answered for the consequences, and my brother and I got by degrees to like him—I by many more degrees than my brother, and with remarkable rapidity.

And he got to like us—to like me especially; and to forget—oh! happy lapse of memory— Matilda.

Before he left Rumney Burn, he asked me to become his wedded wife, and my brother, after some little silent meditation in the summerhouse, started that very day for Southport to make it up with Captain Gray's sister.

PENPRASE THE STONE-BREAKER.

PENPRASE THE STONE-BREAKER.

No, I never thought I should have come down to stone-breaking on a Welsh high-road. In my wildest freaks of imagination—and I had a magnificently freakish imagination once—or in the most hypochondriacal of the moods which would beset me in my advancing years, when fate, destiny. bad luck, call it what you will, got the better of all my far-seeing plans for advancement in the future, I had never pictured to myself a grey-haired, inartistically-clad object at the roadside hammering away at stones. Hanged if I ever guessed it would have come down to that; my jealous and envious friends, relations, and acquaintances, though they had never professed the slightest faith in me, could not believe that I should have descended to it, and thought that I would have preferred to perish by my own hand, just as they would have preferred that wind-up themselves for me, as a more festive and characteristic proceeding on the part of old Paul Penprase.

It is possible that I *had* thought that such a termination to an unfortunate career would be less ignoble than a corner in the white-washed, ill-smelling, disgustingly-ventilated poor-house of Fechenaber; but I had not given up all faith in myself or in my powers, or considered that *this* was the very end of my existence. Not I. I was at seventy-six years of age still looking forward over my heap of cursedly hard flints, over the hills that shut me in with their glaring greens, or their sharp, slatey sides, to the future. Stone-breaking, Fechenaber Workhouse, grim taskmasters, ignorant associates, and the weakest skilly I have ever tasted were only parts of one poor, miserable episode. Great men have had their trials before me, if not quite so late in life; indeed, all great men have had them. And

their chances, too, most of them. I have never
had any chance, though I have looked out for it
pretty sharply in my time, schemed for it, pray-
ed for it, and lied for it. No, not always truthful, I confess. I do not attempt to disguise my
shortcomings here ; it is on account of them that
I have determined to write this story of my
later years. There may be a moral in it somewhere, though I do not see it myself. I was always handy with my pen. There were the
makings of a literary career in me if editors had
condescended to read my manuscripts, if publishers had perused my poems and novels, and
brought them out as they brought out other
people's books ; but I never had my fair chance.
Editors and publishers—I have tried them all—
got weary of me. I palled upon them, and the
only two essays I got into print were found too
closely resembling essays that had already appeared in magazines of bygone days; it was
said that I had copied them *verbatim*. Poor,
half-taught jacks-in-office, who did not know
what *verbatim* meant! I can afford to pity their
ignorance and spite a little now. Let them pass.

They know not—I know not—what they and the world may have lost.

I was handy with my pen, I say again. And when I found that the world of letters was against me, and anxious to trample me under foot, I took to printing tickets for shop-windows and to addressing envelopes for public companies, and so on. There were friends at last who thought they had done me a good turn in securing for me the post of a collector of rates and taxes in the paltry little town of Fechenaber, and they had simply extinguished in me every scrap of ambition and hope of distinction by that process. They had done for me at last—perhaps intentionally, though I make no accusation. I was set in a narrow and sordid-minded groove; I was cribbed, cabined, and confined; there was no poetry of thought in knocking at door after door and being an unwelcome visitor, or told nobody was at home—in taking miserable scraps of money once a quarter, or sueing for those scraps, or threatening distraints, or doing something or other to bring the hatred and contempt of humankind upon me.

I was not fit for a collector's post. I was
told so myself, and by the honourable—the
honourable!—Board of Fechenaber Guardians
later on ; but what I mean is that the height and
depth of my thoughts were so above the petty
tyrannies and harassments of tax-collecting
that my mind was unfitted for it, and became at
last unhinged. That it was unhinged for a
while there can be no doubt, or my accounts
would have been more clear and satisfactory. I
have but little hesitation in asserting that they
were *not* satisfactory to the Board, and that
there were various inquiries, and examinations,
and cross-examinations, and much shaking of
empty heads—terribly empty heads—over my
figures, until I was positively worried half out
of my life—and compelled finally to resign ; and
so the tongue of malevolence was set wagging
in my disfavour, and little boys pointed me out
in the street as the man who had 'sneaked' the
tax-money.

This was my worst time. I did not think
there could have been a lower depth. The
possibilities of getting on after that, and with

the breath of slander circulating even to the
back slums of Fechenaber, were terribly remote;
and it was only gin and a miserable pittance
from my son-in-law, who worked in a quarry till
he was blown to pieces, that kept my spirits up
a bit. They may say I took to drinking at this
time, and to political discussions in the tap-rooms
of the public-houses. They may say what they
like. The utterances of the great unwashed I
have always regarded with supreme indifference:
I have invariably soared above the common
herd. I have known my worth, if other people
have not. I am not the first man who has
wasted his sweetness on the desert air, though I
do not claim just now to being a particularly
sweet old man. I know in my inmost heart that
there are very few wiseacres who could—but this
is not to the purport of my story. Let me get
on.

Despite all my natural gifts, my powers of
speech and language, my perspicacity, my knowledge of the world and of human nature and
the human heart, it came to Fechenaber poorhouse in the long run. Of course my thick-

headed, religious son-in-law said he had warned me it would come to this ; that he had prophesied it all along if I did not work more and talk less ; that I had never looked out for myself, and missed always the main chance; and then *he* died of not looking out when a dynamite charge was going off, and was blown to heaven in little bits, along with the bits of half-a-dozen others that were uncommonly difficult to sort.   People can easily wax eloquent upon the backslidings of other folk ; but Lord, they can slide themselves with anybody, mind you.   I know this, I have seen so much of the world.   I—but I am once more diverging.

I had been in Fechenaber poor-house some three years when the monotony of my life was relieved by a most startling incident in my career.   I had almost settled down to the unalterable; I had become the oracle of the institution, and was generally respected by my contemporaries—an addle-headed lot—although there were a few to carp and snarl at me and my ways, and to taunt me with being a useless, even a snuffy, old dog.

You must not imagine that there are not even in a workhouse envy, hatred, and uncharitableness, jealousy of superior mental attainments, and much barefaced injustice. There is all that, and more.

Why I should for the last six months of my sojourn there have been set to break stones on the various roads leading to Fechenaber, I cannot understand to this day. It was all very well for Davis, the master of the workhouse, to smile and show his teeth and say, 'Penprase, you're a hale old fellow;' I knew that as well as he did, and I did not care for his compliment when it ended in hammering at flints. 'You're looking very well, you're a credit to us; but you must have plenty of fresh air,' the master said; but they said in the house that it was because I had made myself unbearable with my dictatorial airs and nonsensical pompous ways, and that it was a misery to be in my company, and other libels of that kind, for which I could have sued every man jack of them—and, ah, I would have done so too if I had had the means!

No man is to be insulted with impunity in a free and glorious country like this.

Well, it came to stone breaking, to the 'plenty of fresh air,' and the keeping up my constitution, as old Davis ironically put it—I believe he was ironical—and there I was four or five miles from home, day after day of my life, in all weathers—when it rained I was expected to get under a hedge or a haystack,—hammering, pounding, chipping, and very often swearing, when the pieces flew off suddenly and caught me unawares on tender portions of my physiognomy.

Oh, yes, I had plenty of exercise, fresh air, and wet grass; sore places, bronchitis, and rheumatism, and not much sympathy from passers-by. They were not wholly devoid of sympathy, possibly; but, take them for all in all, they were a scaly, shabby, miserable lot. I hated every one of them.

Now and then a carriage would pass, and its inmates look at me in a nasty, superior, supercilious style. More than once I am certain the coachmen have tried to drive over my legs and make an end of me; and the airs people gave themselves—some of those who thought they were honouring me by condescending to address a few words to me—almost made me die of laughing afterwards. There was one ignorant fellow, who had not a 'h' in his whole disposition, but who had made 'his pile' and kept his carriage somehow, who did me the favour of pitying me. I could have smashed his skull in with my hammer.

'Ay, but ye're low down in the wur-r-rld to coom to that, old man,' he said, after bawling in a coarse voice for the coachman to pull up. 'How old are ye?'

'Seventy-six next Michaelmas.'

'It is 'ard lines to be at that work, puir body. 'Ere catch,' and he flipped half-a-crown towards me, right into the long grass—and a nice hunt I had to find it through his clumsiness—and bade his coachman drive on again. Still that was sympathy, though taking a practical and common form, and I make no complaint against it. Had there been more half-crowns flying about

in that fashion I could have born the ignominy
of my position with philosophy. But it was
generally a threepenny piece, and more often
still one of those dix-centimes things that my
tobacconist regards always with grave doubts,
and when in a bad temper will refuse to take.
And oh, the hundreds of people that will pass me
without one glance, despite the woe-begone expression that I *can* assume upon occasion, and
that would melt the heart of any stone less hard
than the accursed specimens heaped up at my
side! Oh, the want of charity in this world!

From the aborigines of this wild part of
Wales I got nothing. 'They knew old Paul too
well,' I heard one scoffer say. Not even a pipe-
ful of tobacco or the loan of a match to light it
with was to be got out of a Welshman. One
man, with his pockets stuffed with tracts, sat beside me once and said he would pray with me,
and I let him do the praying all to himself,
whilst I chopped up stones more savagely than
usual. He remonstrated, especially when he
was hit by one of the bits, and said I was a
hardened old reprobate; and I told him I could

not afford to waste my time, spent in the service
of the State, in listening to him. I could have
argued with him on some points of his discourse,
but he got up and marched away, leaving me
one tract, the grammar of which was awful and
absolutely beneath contempt.

It was in the autumn when I was at work
upon the Plas Chocadoc road—a road extra
hard, and free from sloppiness and muck, and
within a fair distance of the Chocadoc Water-
fall, which fools in summer-time came on coaches
ten and twenty miles to see, even when the
weather was as dry as a chip, and there was
no water to fall from anywhere. It was a dryer,
hotter time for October than had been known
for many years, and well I remember that it
was the hottest and driest of all the days that
had been yet. My hammer sounded like a bell
upon the flints, and the leaves rustled as though
they had been made of metal. It might have
been July or August save for the gold and
copper tints upon the trees, and the absence of
all life upon the mountain roads. Sentimental
idiots said the scenery was sublime about here,

but I had a poor opinion of it myself. Too much up-and-down about it, and too trying to the bunions, God knows, to please me. I was hard to please, I own—men of taste and culture notably are—and despite my surroundings I had never lacked refinement. The scenery was not sublime; it aroused no poetry in me, and its irregularities of surface made me blaspheme a little on my homeward route to Fechenaber.

Sublime or common-place, I had the high-road to myself for hours that day, and I ate the bread and cheese wherewith a beggarly parish had provided me undisturbed by anything save the beastly birds. It was three in the afternoon. One or two market carts, a frowsy old woman knitting as she walked, Sam the grown-up idiot from the next village, dripping at the mouth, and a little boy with a large cow, were all the things and people who had passed me that day. I was tired and hot, and not in too amiable a mood. There are times, even with me, when I am not quite amiable; it is difficult to account for, but let it remain on record. The reader will understand once more that I have

nothing to disguise—that this may be taken
even as a kind of confession, apology, atonement. Yes, atonement if you like—it does not
matter much to me what anybody calls it now.
Kitty—my grand-daughter that is, child of the
silly fellow who blamed me for not looking
about me, and then could not get out of the
way himself of an explosion—wants to see, she
says, what kind of a story I can make out of
it, and so let Kitty have her way for once. She
is not the worst friend I have had in my life,
though she does preach sometimes, and in her
father's style, too, which was always aggravating. But I bear with her; she is very young.

I was not in too amiable a mood, then. It is
possible the weather was unseasonable, and did
not agree with me. I may say conscientiously
that I was not doing my fair amount of work,
and that my labours were self-apportioned on
that particular afternoon, with a due respect
and regard for my advancing years.

I had been dozing. Suddenly, to the left,
and coming up the hill at the top of which I
was at work, I caught sight of a bicyclist ad-

vancing. I detest bicyclists: they are here,
there, and everywhere; they are always in a
hurry, and never have time to put their hands
into their pockets. Theirs is a mean way of
getting along, and I for one despise it. I had
had excellent opportunities of judging of this
class of being since my avocation of stone-
breaking, and I had never known one to throw
me so much as a brass pocket-piece in the whole
course of my professional career. Consequently
I did not love bicyclists—they were objectionable to me; and I should not have even looked
up as he passed me, to see if the rider were young
or old or middling, if he had not come to a full
stop of his own accord and sprung off the bicycle
as he reached me.

'By Jove, your hill is a breather,' he said,
panting as he spoke.

'It isn't my hill,' I answered, shortly enough,
I daresay. I think I have mentioned before
that I was not always as amiable as I might
have been.

'A good thing for you if it were, old man, for
it's all slate, like the mountains yonder.'

'Very likely. It's no business of mine.'

'How far is it to the Chocadoc Falls?'

'A mile-and-a-half.'

'Straight down this hill?'

'Straight on.'

I began to break stones, being tired of his selfish conversation.

He stood by the bicycle, regarding the operation critically. He was a young man, very tall and dark and wiry, and seemed interested in my work. He did not mount his bicycle and ride away; I seemed to have struck his fancy and aroused his interest. He might have seen in me, or in my expression, a something out of the common way. Many people of an observant turn see that immediately. And though I loathe pity, still pity is akin to sixpences, and sixpences buy black shag and cavendish, my favourite 'brands,' though one does not get them good at Fechenaber. Nothing is good there, by the way. A dirty hole of a place.

'It is hard lines for a man of your age,' he said, reflectively, at last. 'Can't they give you something better and easier to do?'

'They could if they liked.   But they won't.'

'Do you come from the Fechenaber—house ?'

'Yes.'

'And have walked all the way ?'

'Yes.'

'And must walk back ?'

'Yes—do you think they send a carriage for me ?'

'They will some day—a black one—if they keep you long at this game,' he said, indignantly. Then he added : 'But never mind; at least you get away from depressing surroundings to the sunshine.'

'And hard work.'

'Oh, you don't like work?' he asked, drily.

'I said hard work : manual work, I mean.'

'You're not used to it ?'

'I have been only used to it since I went into the house.'

'Tell us all about it, old gentleman.'

He wheeled his bicycle to the side, laid it gingerly against the hedge-bank, sat down on the heap of stones, and began to light his pipe. A cool customer, I could see now ; but it would lead to some miserly but ostentatious dole, and it would be etiquette to change my keynote and be friendly.

'Have some baccy,' he said, slangily, and pitched his tobacco pouch at me and laughed. He was too fond of laughing at anything and everything, to my fancy; but then life was more of a joke with him than with me, and he had a lot of go in him. When people have too much go in them, they always grin. I took his tobacco and filled my short pipe. I was not too proud for that; it was offered in good fellow-ship; there was no more patronage about the offer than he could help.

'What have you been doing all your long life, to wind up with stone-breaking in the Chocadoc road?'

He was very curious and persistent, and I could not make him out. As a rule, I sum up people pretty quickly, and read their characters like books; but this young fellow bothered me. He was too free-and-easy, too familiar altogether. presumed on the difference between his position and mine, his age and mine; and yet he did it all in a way I could not take offence at. He was not an excursionist, 'a tripper' from Liverpool, a Lancashire lad whose father had made money in cotton, a shopman out for a holiday, or anything of that sort; and if he had been a gentleman, born and bred, he would not have kept grinning and chuckling at everything I said. Certainly I was amusing enough, and when I saw that my satirical remarks were quickly seized upon and enjoyed I knew that this young man had a keen appreciation of humour—which is a great gift. I never possessed that. In all my life I have never seen anything to laugh at. I told him so, as a hint that his exuberance of spirits was a *leetle* bit offensive; but he only laughed the more, so I did not put him down for quite the gentleman—only a half-and-half, with a good deal of froth on the top, that required blowing away before you could get to anything sensible.

As he appeared particularly struck with me, I was communicative enough. I told him the whole of my career; I thought it was as well he should know it—that it would be worth my while—and that, at any rate, it was better occupation than breaking-up stones. It was a long story, but it did not tire him. It was a compliment to the powers of my narrative that he seemed to forget all about the Chocadoc Falls; he listened to every word with great attention—I do not remember ever meeting with a listener half as patient; but if he had been more touched by my misfortunes he would have shown more delicacy of feeling. On the contrary, he laughed, as I have said already. Other people's troubles, trials, and disappointments seemed to amuse him wonderfully; and when I told him of my literary gifts, my compositions, and my struggles to be famous, he lay on his back on the stones and roared till the tears ran out of his eyes.

'I don't see anything to make quite such a row over,' I said at last, severely. I could stand a good deal when a half-a-crown was looming in the distance; but his irreverence and his want of respect and kindly sympathy were too much for my composure.

'I beg pardon, Mr. Penprase, I'm sure,' he

said, sitting up and wiping his eyes with his pocket-handkerchief, 'but I can't help it, upon my honour. I'm glad I've met you. You're about as droll an old——' and then off he went again almost into hysterics, and I wished he were a flint and I could crack him.

However, all's well that ends well, the bard says. He gave me a sovereign as a wind-up. I was pretty fairly astonished—that *douceur* made amends for all his boisterousness and ill-timed hilarity. It was a princely gift—it meant a lot to me. For the first time in my life, too, I felt a throb of gratitude, the gift was so gracefully bestowed. It was not displayed in a look-here kind of way; it was not chucked at me; it was passed into my palm, and my own fingers pressed over it so sharply that he hurt me; he did not wish me to see what it was until he had mounted his bicycle and was off out of earshot of my thanks. Indeed, I thought it *was* a shilling, and had not said a word—not even responded 'Good day' to his parting salutation to me as he rattled away down the hill towards Chocadoc.

Then, when I had realised my good fortune, I

did run to the brow of the hill and call out 'God bless you, sir!' and wave my old workhouse cap, and flourish my hammer, and dance like an old lunatic in the middle of the road. He did not look round, but went on at a break-neck rate down the steepest hill in all South Wales, at a rate which was enough to bring any bicycle and its rider to summary grief, as at this rate of his it did completely.

He was not prepared for the stones I had spread myself last week over the road, and close to the bottom of the hill; he had been prepared for the steep descent it was; and though warned by his extra rate of progression he was not inclined, being headstrong, to take his warning and act with anything like discretion, but dashed on at his old mad pace, until he and his bicycle together were hurled on one side, and crumpled up and smashed in a single instant, and whilst I was looking after him. It was like a flash of lightning, and then all so tremendously still! I stood and stared before me; there was no movement, no cry for help, not a single sound anywhere. It was as though I had dreamt it all, if it had not been for the broken and twisted wheels in the distance, and the dark still object mixed up with them, and which I knew to be a man.

I pitched my long hammer on to the stones I had been breaking, and set off down the hill as fast as my rheumatic limbs would carry me. Heavens, what a way he had got! what a long hill it was! I had never thought much of the distance before. It seemed as if I should never get to him—that my legs would never keep me up all the way.

I was stooping over him at last. Yes, there he was, with all the laugh out of him, and his face bloody and hard and rigid, and an ugly wound in his forehead, and his eyes shut, and God knows with what limbs broken. Not that that mattered much, I thought at once, for he was surely dead. There was not any doubt about it. 'Dead and gone that man!' I muttered; 'and only talking to me full of life just three minutes ago!' It was shocking, wonderful, exciting. There would be an inquest, and I should be the principal witness in the case, the principal character in the tragedy—bar the dead man, of course. And I should be paid extra expenses, and made much of for a while, and my name would be in all the Welsh papers: 'Paul Penprase, a highly intelligent witness, who gave his evidence with much intelligence and graphic force'—that is how it would probably run.

I put my hand upon his heart, but I could not feel it beating; there was no pulsation at the wrist; there were dark death-rings underneath the eyes already; he was in such an awkward heap that I began to wonder what kind of coffin he would require if they could not straighten him out a bit before he stiffened into a star-fish kind of pattern. I put my hand upon his heart again. Yes, dead—how could there be a doubt about it? Very dead indeed.

What to do with him, and how to let people know, was not at once clear to me. It was five miles back to Fechenaber, and not so much as a cottage on the way; it was about the same distance on past Chocadoc, with no house on the road that I could call to mind; and to stand

still and holloa was to look like a fool, and do
no good, and spoil my voice. I ran all this
over in my mind, with my hand upon his heart,
and upon a big watch which he had in the
breast-pocket of his braided bicycle-jacket.
When I was sure his heart did not beat, I became certain that his watch did—I could hear
it ticking. I thought that I should like to know
the time when this accident had happened. I
should be sure to be asked that question at the
inquest.

I drew forth his watch—a massive gold
hunter, to which a gold chain and seals were
attached—a handsome but rather vulgar-look-
ing watch, and with the initials J. W. L. flourishing all over the back of it in diamonds. A
little too flashy this, and in execrable taste, but
still too valuable an affair to be left in the pocket
of a man lying dead by the roadside, and where
I should have to leave him whilst I went to tell
the news and get assistance.

Why tell the news and get assistance at all?
Why not let somebody else find this poor unlucky traveller, and so be quit of all the fuss

and bother of it? The man being dead, it could not matter who discovered him, and some tramp would have been supposed to see him first, and help himself to what the pockets of the gentleman contained. It would save me a lot of trouble—and I had never liked trouble—if I let this awkward matter alone. True, I was stone-breaking on the road that day; but then I had left early—was taken ill or something—and had gone back to the house. There would be no difficulty about evading that part of the subject. What else had he got in his pocket? Money, of course, or he would not have been so free with his sovereigns. I had better see.

I was about to see, when his eyes opened suddenly, as though he were mechanical and I had touched a spring, and he lay and stared at me most uncomfortably. I thought I should have dropped upon my knees with fright, he glared so.

'Water!' he gasped out at last—'wa—ter!'

'Yes; I'll get it, from the Falls. It's a blessed long way, though, down the valley. Do you think you really care about it?'

'Wa—ter!'

'I shall be gone half-an-hour, or three-quarters; I don't think it's worth your waiting all that time for: you'll be dead before I get back.'

'Water!' he moaned again, and he looked so queerly at me that I went. I had slung round my little can, that had had cold tea in it—at least, they always called it tea at Fechnaber poorhouse, but it might just as well have been called a hair-wash—and it would be easy to fill the can when I got to the stream—that stream which the Falls fed, and which was such a confoundedly long way off.

But I should be rewarded by the young gentleman's friends and executors; I should have done my duty; I should have saved his watch from being stolen; I should have acted altogether the good Samaritan. I went across the fields—field after field, and all down-hill—I did not guess what the coming up again would cost me. I got excited, and began to run and stumble, when I heard the waters in the distance murmuring, splashing, roaring as they leaped over the black rocks, and went headlong down

forty feet into the boulder-strewn brook below
—the brook to which I was advancing gingerly,
sliding down to amidst a wilderness of bracken
and bramble.

I reached the stream, filled my tin can, and
prepared to re-ascend. No, I had not calculated
on the trouble it would be to me to get to the
level of the high-road again. I had not made
sufficient allowance for my old age and shaky
knees and paucity of breath. It was the task
of a Hercules to work one's way through that
stiff ascent of underwood, with the brambles
catching at every turning and hooking small
pieces of my wardrobe from me, and running
into my flesh and wounding me. I thought I
should die before I got to the top, and so get
the start of the young fool who had sent me on
such an errand and be in heaven before him.
I could fancy his surprise at finding I was there
already, and I wondered if he would ask me
first thing if I had got his watch safe, or could
tell him what the time was?

I was hot and sick and puffy, and red as fire
with constant rushes of blood to the head, and

at every step that I dragged upwards I cursed
the folly which had placed me in this absurd
position.   If I had thought for a moment or two,
I must have guessed that the bicyclist *must* be
dead before I got back, and it would have been
easy to sit down and wait quietly till it was all
over.   But my impulsive nature had taken me
to the stream, and here was I crawling on my
stomach like a lizard, trying to get back again,
and feeling fit to die, and swearing horribly.   I
blush now to think of the oaths that escaped
my lips with every fleeting breath; but I had
been unused to this kind of exertion, had never
laid myself out for it, and found that it was
doing its best to kill me.

I think I must have lost consciousness at last,
for I lay on my tin can and made an effort to
get up and crawl the rest of the way to the
wounded man.   I was done for, if I did not
take care.   I was nearly at my last gasp; self-
preservation *was* the first law of nature, and he
had better do his last gasp than I.   It was all
his fault, dashing down the hill like the maniac

that he was.   Why should I kill myself for him?
What was he to me?

But when I had recovered my breath I
gathered myself together, and crawled upwards
the rest of the way.   I got to the high-road
again; the Lord knows how long I had been
gone, but the sun was going down sharpish behind the slate hills, and there were grey
shadows on the landscape.   And in the high-
road, where I had left the wounded man and his
shattered bicycle, there remained no trace of
either—everything had been cleared off—and it
was all like a dream.

.   .   .   .

For days and days, for weeks and weeks
afterwards I tired out my brains in wondering
what had become of the man I had left for dead
on the Chocadoc road.   *Was* he dead? and had
he been carted away?   Had he recovered—was
it possible he had recovered after such a terrible
crumpling up, and walked off with the fragments
of the bicycle under his arm?   Had he been
picked up by passers-by whilst I was absent, and
if so where had they carried him?   Had some

tramp seen him, and finished him surely for the sake of the purse of money he might have had, and dragged him amongst the ferns and black-berry bushes, where he might lie for weeks un-discovered? Had I really dreamt it all, and there had been no accident whatever? Had my brain given way beneath the occupation of stone-smashing, and this was my first delusion as a neat start off? I could have believed these two last solutions to the mystery had it not been for the decisive reality of the watch. I had the watch; it was a tangible fact. It *was* a beauty!

And what to do with it? There was the trouble and the uncertainty. To tell the master of the workhouse was to have his officious paws on it in his extreme anxiety to take care of it, to lock it away from me, to advertise it in the newspapers, to get it, by hook or by crook, out of my possession, to wait till I was dead and stick to it! I could not trust anybody, I never did trust anybody; why should I trust him? Was I not able to manage my own affairs better than other people could manage them for me?

Had I not more forethought than the poor ignorant hirelings by whom I was surrounded?

I would wait. Everything comes to him who waits, they say, even gold watches with monograms in diamonds on their backs. I should hear of the man presently, and failing to hear of him in a year or two—say in a month or two—one might reasonably presume that the watch would never be inquired for. But what *had* become of him?

I looked in the *Fechenaber Observer* every week—I could always get a glimpse of that badly conducted periodical—for an account of an 'accident to a tourist.' Never a word. I read the contents-bills of all the other papers outside the stationers' shops; there was not a line in big type recording any disaster on the Chocadoc road. All kinds of accidents except the accident that had happened to him.

There were no advertisements for missing property either, no rewards offered for the recovery of a valuable gold chronometer. I had to look at that watch twenty times a day to make sure that I had really got it. I cannot assert that it was a comfortable acquisition; I had to keep it loose in my trousers pocket like an apple, and to sleep with it at the bottom of the bed like a foot-warmer; I was always in dread of its being discovered on me, of my being regarded as a receiver of stolen goods—of my being remanded at police-courts until inquiries were made, and the inquiries bringing the owner forward with his whole story, which he, if of an imaginative turn of mind, could twist round to my disadvantage. There were times when I thought it would be better to sell it and have done with it; but a man in the infamous livery of Fechenaber workhouse offering for sale a watch and chain of that description seemed too suggestive of robbery and murder for a sane man to risk. I would wait a little longer.

I believe the possession of the watch, and the constant workings of an overwrought mind as to what had become of the missing man, stretched me at last upon a sick-bed. I felt it coming on by degrees, so I had time to prepare for the crisis. I was sure that it would not do for the watch to be discovered in my possession

whilst I lay defenceless in bed, so I went out
for the last bit of stone-breaking I felt I should
do for a long time, put the watch and chain in
my tobacco-pouch, wrapped the tobacco-pouch
in last week's *Observer*, spat on the lot for luck,
and buried my treasure under a big beech-tree,
which had been struck by lightning years ago,
and which lay to the right of the third milestone from Fechenaber.   And then I went back
to the poorhouse and took to my bed like a
lamb.

It was only my usual winter's complaint—
rheumatics and that kind of thing allied to a
compound wheeze; but I had had it—oh, nice
and regularly—every winter, and was pretty
well prepared for it.   I was sorry it had come
on earlier than usual, and so were the people at
the house, because I had rather more of their
company, and they had rather more of mine,
than was altogether conducive to perfect harmony between us.   I never could get on with
them long together—they were not of my mental calibre.   There was nothing in common between us but our poverty; and as for the infir-

mary nurses and the master of the house, they were as ignorant a lot as one might naturally expect in such an out-of-the-way corner of South Wales as Fechenaber was.

It was a very sharp turn at last with me, for I turned the corner by the merest shave. I was so sure that I was marked out for a premature decease, and that the world would find out too late what a man it had had in its midst and cruelly ignored, that the watch got upon my mind again, and I talked in my sleep so much about it, and the diamonds on the back, and J. W. L., and milestones and beech-trees, that they shaved my head to keep me cool and comfortable. I sent for my granddaughter when I was at my worst. Kitty and I had not agreed very well of late days; she had married without my consent a hulking brute of a dock labourer, who did menial work about the harbour at Borthmouth, and I had expressed myself forcibly upon the disgrace to the Penprases such a match had been, and we had not spoken since the marriage. But one forgets family feuds when the breath is short and there is a rattle in the throat; at least I did, not being a malicious man. Besides, there were a watch and chain hidden under a beech-tree three miles from Fechenaber, and I did not want any property of mine to go out of the family—to lie idle for ever and ever under the ground like my very unfortunate self.

Kitty responded to my call, and, much to my surprise and vexation, she brought her husband with her. I did not want to see him; he was essentially a vulgar man, with a voice like a bull of Bashan's and a fist like a shoulder of mutton. He was one of your big men, and big men have always been my abomination. They have never any intellect. I am small myself; so was Napoleon, Nelson, Victor Hugo—were not they?—and a great many more that I could mention if I had the time to recollect them. I do not quite know how it is, but I always distrust a big man. I distrusted Thomas Griffiths, and when they came I did not breathe a syllable about the watch and chain, and I think they wondered why I had sent a message in such a tremendous hurry, saying that I was ill and had something particular to say before I died, and then only lay and coughed at them for an hour-and-a-half. Kitty was very much distressed at my condition, as well she might be, and cried a great deal, as well she might do, considering how she had neglected me and failed to appreciate me.

'He's the only relation I have in the world, Tom.' she sobbed.

Tom looked as if he thought that was an advantage rather than otherwise if I were to be taken as a sample, but he had the common decency to keep his mouth shut. But I could read him well enough. I knew what was passing in his mind, for all his bovine stare at me.

'I'm sure this nasty workhouse is killing him, Tom. To think that my own and only grandfather should have to die in the Union!" she went on.

'There's many a better nor him have had to come to it,' was the brute's answer; 'it looks comfor'ble and clean.'

'It's the air and the position that's preying

on him. But grandfather always was so—so—
so——'

'Stuck up?' suggested her husband.

'Proud like. And he was clever too—very.
Oh, Tom,' she cried, 'don't you think we could
take care of the poor old fellow till he died!'

'I don't mind,' he said; 'if it please you,
lass, have him. It isn't nice sartinly'—he always said 'sartinly'—'to have to own the parish
planted the poor old boy.'

'And I might nurse him and bring him round
again. Who knows?' she said.

Tom did not seem to regard this point of
view with as much favour as the last suggestion,
but he did not make any comment upon it.
Bringing me round had, I daresay, to his little
mind, its drawbacks.

They had their way. I let them have it.
They carried me from Fechenaber to Borthmouth, where Kitty did the nursing very well.
I had nothing to complain about except the
weak character of the beef-tea, and the noise
her husband made, tramping in and out of the
place in iron-cased boots that shook the whole

house like a jelly. Kitty brought me round, as she had thought she might do.

Thus I was free of the poorhouse and of stone-breaking in my latter days; and Kitty bought me a whole ream of paper and a box of pens, and sat me by the side of the fire, and said,

'Now write, grandfather, something that shall astonish us at last.'

'It will keep him quiet, at any rate,' her husband said, gruffly, and I did not thank him for the observation. Keep me quiet indeed! As if I made one quarter of the thundering row which he did upon the premises.

My granddaughter had some of the family pride in her—on her mother's side, of course.

'I hope you will not say anything about Fechenaber poorhouse, grandad,' she said to me one day. 'There's no occasion you should own to that, and lower us.'

'I'll never mention it, Kitty,' was my promise to her. Not that I should have been likely to mention it. Why, everybody in Borthmouth thought that I lived most of my time in London, engaged in literary pursuits. I had told them so myself. No one could have dreamt that a man of my general appearance and attainments had broken stones on the Fechenaber road, or that I knew as much as where the road was. And that road was troubling me. I wanted to be on it, and to get my hidden treasure into my own hands again. It would be more easy to dispose of in this neighbourhood; some master-skipper might take a fancy to it, and give me a round sum down, without asking any questions. What was the use of my treasure to me when I had not benefited one farthing by it? I had kept it long enough for the rightful owner to turn up and claim it surely. Then why didn't he? But what excuse could I make to get towards Fechenaber, and how was I to raise the capital to meet the expenses of the journey? Tom Griffiths was a covetous sort of man, and kept me cruelly short of pocket-money.

'You can jog along if I find you in bacca, dad,' he said; and so I jogged along without much thanks to him.

I had been about eight months with the Griffithses, when a chance seemed to present itself of getting Fechenaber way. Some people in the town were moving in that direction—shopkeepers who supplied me with stationery—and their goods and chattels were to go by road and take two days. It was summer-time again, and I suggested that I thought that the ride and change of air, and the violent exercise of hanging on to the tail-board of a van without springs, would do me good. So it was settled, though it was not a journey that was ever to come off.

The day before the expedition I was at the extreme end of the stone jetty, or harbour, as they please to call it, ostensibly watching the fishing-boats come in, but planning out my scheme to reach the stricken beech-tree on the high-road without arousing the suspicions of those by whom I should be accompanied.

It was nearly sunset, and a fine, calm, evening. I was looking out to sea, with my back to the town and to the jetty along which I had come for a breath of fresh air. The Griffiths's house was always uncommonly stuffy. I knew somebody was advancing by the rattle of heels upon the cobble stones, but I did not look round. I was not curious to know who it was. Very likely it might be Tom Griffiths come to fetch me home, and put me to bed like a baby. They treated me like a child—and that was another drop in the cup of bitterness, which I had to quaff to the brim.

Yes—it was Tom Griffiths, but not alone. There was a stranger with him—a young man in a dark blue suit, I saw when I turned round at their call.

'Daddy,' said Tom, 'here's a gentleman been all over Borthmouth inquiring for you. Here he is, sir,' to the gentleman; 'that's Mr. Penprase.'

I thought I should have slid off my stone post into the sea when I saw who it was. My head swam, and my eyes tried to pop out of my head, and my heart went galloping on anyhow. It was the man who had come to grief on the Chocadoc road twelve months ago!

He walked up to me and faced me. He had not altered much since I had seen him last, and there was the same ridiculous inclination to burst out laughing which I had noticed last time. There was an ugly scar in the middle of his forehead, which one could see very distinctly, as he wore a straw hat on the extreme back of his head, like a 'silly Charlie.'

'Mr. Penprase,' he said, 'I am very glad to find you. I had almost given up the hope of ever coming across you again. How are you?'

I did not answer. My thoughts did not flow as rapidly as they used when I was writing for the magazines. I wanted time for cool reflection.

'Don't you know me,' he added.

'I never set eyes on you in all my life before,' I said, with a vacant stare at him.

'You *don't* know me?'

'No.'

'Don't you remember my meeting with an accident on the Chocadoc road?'

'I never saw anybody meet an accident, It's time enough for an accident when it comes, isn't it?'

He threw his head back and laughed again.

'Ah! you are a sharp old boy—I remember. My memory is better than yours, you see. You

were breaking stones on the high-road when I
first saw you.'

'Doing what?'

'Breaking stones.'

'I've had my trials, but I've never come down
to that.   Only workhouse people break stones.'

'Well, you'd come from the workhouse at
Fechenaber.   You said so yourself.'

'I never heard tell of such a place.'

The man looked puzzled—as well he might.
I did it very well.   I was on my guard now,
and acted to the life.   I have often thought I
should have made a most excellent actor had I
ever had the chance.

'Your name *is* Penprase?'

'That's my name, sure enough.   I don't deny
that.'

'It's not a common name.'

'There are plenty of that name in these
parts.'

'And you're not the Penprase who was laid
up last winter in the infirmary of Fechenaber
poorhouse?' he asked, to my surprise.   He had
been there after me, the sneak—he had been

scouring South Wales for me.   I must keep to
my own story at any cost till I had time to think
what was best to be done.

'No,' I answered, 'I am not that Penprase.'

'Gosh!' suddenly cried out that stupid ass
Griffiths.

'What's the matter with *you*?' asked the
young man, wheeling himself round, and looking up into Tom's face.

'Left—pipe—at home,' said Tom, who could
tell a lie sharp enough when he liked; and
away he clattered down the pier as hard as he
could go, and left us both—as he owned afterwards—'to fight it out atwixt us.'   Which was
mean of him.

What protection had I, if this stranger were
suddenly to lose his temper and tell me I was
a thief?   I looked after Tom—I called after
him, but he did not or he would not hear me;
and there was I left alone with my persecutor—
perhaps my prosecutor presently—who could
tell?   I broke into a cold perspiration at the
very thought of it.   Why, the man might begin
bawling for a policeman within the next five

minutes; he had left off that silly grin of his, and was regarding me now gravely.

'You have been ill, haven't you?' he asked, when we were alone together.

'I don't know that I have.'

'Your grandson-in-law owned as much as that. Since you have been here, I mean?' he said.

'I'm an old man, and likely to feel queerish now and then. What are you asking me all these questions for?'

'I thought perhaps your memory might have gone lately. I hope it has.'

'That's very kind of you,' I replied, 'but it's as good as ever it was.'

'And yet you do not remember my spill on the road near the Chocadoc Falls, and your running off to get water—and whilst you were running a cart came by and took me and my broken traps off to the first doctor—and a deuce of a long way off he lived. But—he patched me up.'

'I'm sorry to hear you have been hurt, young man,—but—I don't know anything about you.'

'I should have come to Fechenaber to see you as soon as I got well—but my leave was up and I had to join my ship. It's only lately that I have got back to Wales and managed to get this way again.'

'What did you want to see me for—or the poor pauper that you take for me?' I asked.

I thought I must ask that question, though I was afraid of what was coming and knew—as I thought—what would be his answer. But he took my breath away by saying,

'To reward the old man for all the trouble he took to get life into me. To thank him for the run he had for the water which I never stopped to drink. And by Jove it must have been a run! I have been to that break-neck valley since, and it's a rare up and down and it takes it out of a fellow.'

'It's a dreadful place——'

'Eh?'

'I have heard,' I concluded. 'I don't know anything about it personally.'

'Well, then, I won't take up your time any longer, Mr. Penprase.'

'Thankee.'

'Yours is a wonderful likeness to the other gentleman at the Union; and you—but it *is* getting late.   By Jove, it must be close upon eight o'clock.'

He drew from his pocket a handsome gold chronometer—*the* chronometer!—with the J.W.L. in diamonds flashing at the back.   I could have sworn to it anywhere.   I was never more completely taken off my guard; my knees knocked together, and my white hair seemed stiffening into wires.

'Where the devil did you get that?' I shrieked out.   That's mine!'

'Is your name James Walter Lidgey, or Paul Penprase?'

'Penprase; but, for God's sake, tell me how you got that watch.   Give it me : it's mine! it's mine!'

I was beside myself; I was showing my hand now; I was jumping head first into the trap.   I was an old fool.

'This can't be yours,' he said; 'this was stolen from me when I lay helpless on the Chocadoc road. It was a watch given to me by one whose life I had saved at sea. and I treasure it very much. When I came back from my last voyage, I thought I would find you out and ask if you knew anything about it. I was certain that some one had robbed me, and, though I was sorry, I fancied it must be you.'

'Oh! I looked like a thief, I suppose. Go on,' I said.

' You had told me you were in the poorhouse, and I went to look for you there. You had left. Then I found out the parish doctor and he gave me your address. I inquired into your case, and he said you were a rum old stick.'

' He was a disrespectful hound. But he was always like that.'

'He told me that you had been very ill—completely off your head at last, and raved of nothing but your own cleverness, gold watches, milestones, and the beech-tree that was struck by lightning on the Fechenaber road. I put this and that together ; I went carefully along the road and found a tree that had been struck by lightning near the third milestone from the town. I guessed that you had buried the property there. I had half-an-hour's digging with a garden trowel, and found a watch along with some other things which don't belong to me. I have left a tobacco-pouch and a few things, on your mantelpiece at home, Mr. Penprase, if they're any good to you now.'

I did not say any more. I did not know what to say. It was a complete checkmate to me, and I was powerless. If I had been a younger man, I should have punched his head, I dare say, or showed a clean pair of heels down the causeway, and out of the town—probably done the latter as less embarrassing. But I was old; I had been ill; I was very feeble and at his mercy, and he took every advantage of my mental prostration. It did not strike me that he was one who would make an example of me—only an artful fellow who had got the better of me. Not a stern and rigid individual, or he would not have been able to laugh at everything so much.

And he began laughing again when I took my handkerchief out to wipe my eyes.

'There, poor old beggar,' he said. 'We'll say no more about it.'

'I saved your life, sir,' I said, making no attempt to disguise facts any more.

'Well, perhaps you did. And you took care of my watch too—and would have told me all about it, and where it was hidden if I had not taken you so much off your guard. Eh, Paul Penprase?'

'Yes—I think—I should have told you—in time.'

'I will try and think so. I hope you will try too—for you are a very old man and——'

'Not so very old, sir. And I've got all my faculties about me still.'

'One or two faculties too many,' he said, laughing; and I have often wondered what he meant by that, 'but you are old.'

'I am not a young man certainly.'

'Try to see the matter in the right light, before you get much older, Penprase,' he said, 'it won't do you any harm when you come to the flat of your back again, with not too much time to think it over. Good evening.'

And away he went without giving me so much as a sixpence for taking care of all that property which he must have lost if it had not been for me.   There is no end of ingratitude in this world.   I have seen a lot of it in my time, goodness knows.

THE END.

LONDON: PRINTED BY DUNCAN MACDONALD, BLENHEIM HOUSE.